THE
Highland Escape

Copyright © 2024 by Emily Silver

All rights reserved.

This is a work of fiction. Names, characters, places and incidents are either the product of the author's imagination or are use fictitiously. Any resemblance to actual persons, living or dead, businesses, companies, events or locations is entirely coincidental.

No part of this book may be reproduced in any form or by any electronic or mechanical means, including information storage and retrieval systems, without written permission from the author, except for the use of brief quotations in a book review. For more information, please email the author at Emily@authoremilysilver.com.

Cover Design by Star Child Designs

Editing by Happily Editing Anns

www.authoremilysilver.com

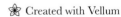 Created with Vellum

THE HIGHLAND ESCAPE

EMILY SILVER

To Scotland
Thanks for inspiring this trip and being so amazing

A Note From The Author

Hey there!

I'm so happy you picked up The Highland Escape. I love Kirby and Callum and hope you do too! As a note, Scottish English is used in this book. It's gone through edits and a beta reader from Scotland, so those aren't typos, they are supposed to be there, aye?

Some examples:
- Dinnae - do not/don't
- Didnae - did not/didn't
- Disnae - does not/doesn't
- Cannae- can't
- Couldnae- couldn't
- Winnae- won't
- Widnae- wouldn't
- Huvnae- haven't
- Hasnae- hasn't
- Isnae- isn't
- Wasn't- wisnae

Happy reading!
    <3 Emily

Chapter One

KIRBY

Today's the day. The day I've been waiting for. The biggest moment of my entire career—the promotion that I've been wanting since I started my job with Thompson and Associates right after graduating from college. I've been working my way up the chain ever since.

Is working for a shipping logistics company the dream? No.

But getting to become the VP of my department before I turn thirty? Yes.

It's not even six a.m. when I'm pushing open the door to the building and making my way toward my small office.

The walls are a stark white, showcasing the various awards and certifications I've gotten over the years. Two black leather chairs sit in front of an all glass desk. The windows face downtown LA and the traffic that is starting to pick up, even at this early hour. The only personal item is a photo of me and my mom when I graduated from college.

From day one, my boss told me it was all business. That

I'm not here to make friends. I've taken that to heart. Work is everything to me. It's been my life the last eight years—forgoing most personal relationships to get ahead.

Slipping out of my black trench coat, I hang it and my briefcase in the small closet and turn on my computer.

The blinking countdown is a reminder of what this day holds.

Breathe, Kirby. It will all be okay. You're made for this job.

With half of our company in Europe and the Pacific, dozens of emails await me. I fire off responses and start making calls with trained efficiency. I could do this job in my sleep.

Imports and duty fees. Shipping routes. Changes in laws.

All of it requires my full dedication, one hundred percent of the time.

"Hey." Joanne, one of my few friends here, pops her head into my office. The morning has gone by in the blink of an eye. "Want to grab lunch?"

Glancing at the clock that hangs in my bare office, I grab my purse. "Sure. But can we make it quick? I want to be back here in enough time for my meeting."

The only thing that matters today is my meeting with the president and COO. If it weren't for Joanne, I'd probably sit at my desk and work through lunch.

"I know." Joanne rolls her eyes at me. "This is the only thing you've talked about for the last two months."

Smiling at her, I follow her out of the office and down the street to our favorite café. It's a health lover's dream. Everything from green smoothies to tofu to anything vegan you can find.

We love it because they have the fastest service time. In our fast-paced world, every minute counts.

Joanne and I each order our usual salads and take a seat by the window. Green metal chairs scuff against the hardwood floors. Fair trade posters line the wall and greenery hangs in baskets around us. People come and go as easy chatter hangs in the air.

"Do you still want to get drinks tonight?" Joanne asks, cracking open her water bottle and taking a gulp.

"Nothing to celebrate yet," I tell her. "I don't want to jinx it."

She waves me off in a perfume of Chanel N° 5. "All anyone ever talks about is how great Kirby is. How dedicated she is to her job. Why can't employees be more like her. If you don't get it, I'll chew my arm off."

"Please don't do that." Our salads are set down in front of us. "We'll celebrate once we have something to celebrate."

"I'm getting the first round."

I can't help my smile. Joanne was one of my first friends here and has been my closest confidante ever since. Even though I've lived in LA my entire life, I don't have a lot of girlfriends. Most of them either have kids or have moved away. And with my work schedule, it doesn't leave a lot of time for catching up.

Joanne is the one person who at least tries to make sure I don't get too caught up in work.

"Earth to Kirby." Joanne snaps her fingers in front of my face. "I can see you starting to stress."

"Sorry." I shake off my stupor, stabbing my fork into the giant bowl of leafy greens sitting in front of me. I'm too nervous to eat anything else. "I'm trying not to worry, but you know how it is."

"You're a shoo-in. I don't know why you're so worried."

"And so is Glenn. He's put in just as much work as I have and he's been with the company longer."

"So?" Joanne shrugs a shoulder. "You work on more complex accounts. That has to count for something."

"We'll see. I can't think about this any more than I already am, so tell me about your new guy."

A blush creeps up her cheeks as she delves into all the details of her latest dating conquest. I live vicariously through her. Where Joanne spends her weekends meeting all kinds of new people, my weekends are spent at the office.

By the time we're done with lunch, I could practically tell you her new guy's kindergarten teacher's name as we head back to the office. Joanne links arms with me as we tap our badges at the security turnstiles and head toward the elevators.

She turns to face me as we wait for the elevator to take us to our floor. "Everything is going to be fine. When you take over the entire company in two years, I can say I knew you when."

I give her the best smile I can. One that is full of nerves and excitement. "Thank you."

She gives me a quick hug before the elevator car opens and we head up. We each go our separate ways, and the time before my meeting is spent pacing in my office. I get little done before I'm heading down to the large conference room.

Ross, a fit, older man in his sixties, welcomes me in. The HR director is also there. She's a hard woman—never offering a smile to anyone. I'm not sure why she's here instead of the COO. Maybe she's here to expedite processing my promotion?

I can only hope.

"Ross. Beth. How are you today?" I say politely, taking

a seat across from both of them. A pitcher of water and three glasses sit in the center of the black table. The Thompson and Associates emblem hangs on the wall, like a reminder of why we're all here.

"Kirby. I wish we were having this meeting under better circumstances."

My brow furrows at Ross's words. I cross one leg over the other and drape my folded hands onto the table in front of me. "I'm sorry—better circumstances?"

"Are you aware of the recent changes to the Muller account?"

I try to rack my brain for who they are. It doesn't sound like anyone I've worked with. "I'm not, no."

Ross and Beth eye one another before pulling a piece of paper from the stack sitting in front of them and handing it over to me.

"Do you recognize this?"

It's a list of import fees and duties. Something I review daily. But something is off. Knowing what I do about these different areas, the fees are higher than they should be.

"What am I looking at?"

"Why don't you tell us?"

Dropping the paper onto the desk, I eye the two people in front of me. "Seeing as how I don't know this account, could you explain to me what is going on?"

I try to keep the frustration out of my voice, but this day is taking a turn and I don't know if I'm going to like the direction it's headed.

"Someone has been charging our customer more in duties and import fees than they should and skimming the difference off the top," Ross says. His voice is firm, almost accusatory, and it has a lead weight dropping into my stomach.

"Wait, you don't think I did this, do you?"

"As you can see here,"—Beth hands over a stack of papers—"all of these were done under your direction."

I rip the stack from her with more force than necessary to see my sign-off on this account. My mind is spinning, trying to figure out what is going on.

"I don't work with Muller. That region falls under Tony's area."

Ross points a finger at me. "You still have access to the documents. The only question we can't figure out is why."

"Why?" My head is swirling with confusion.

Beth gives me a curt nod. "Why you would skim money off the top of one of our top grossing customers."

"But I'm not!" I shout. "There's no reason why I would do it."

"Did you need the money?" Ross asks. "You could have come to us if you were having problems."

"I'm not, though."

I'm trying to glean what I can from the numbers on the page as fast as I can, but Beth pulls them out of my hands. It's small amounts here and there and then bigger amounts. Whoever did this knew what they were doing.

"There will be an investigation."

"Wait. Investigation?" My mouth is dry and my blood runs cold. "This is a mistake."

Ross stiffens, pushing his glasses farther up his nose. "I assure you, Kirby, there is no mistake. The records are clear."

"But…can I see them?"

Ross shakes his head. "There will be an investigation, and should charges need to be filed, they will be."

"Charges?"

My mind is spinning. I walked in here not ten minutes ago assuming I'd get the promotion I've been wanting since I started here. That I've given up everything to achieve. Now? Now, I'm under investigation for something I didn't do.

"Security will see you out."

Two men in dark suits appear at the door. "Are you kidding me? I don't even get to defend myself?"

"There will be the opportunity for that at the conclusion of our investigation."

"I can't believe this," I mutter to myself. "After everything I've given to this company, this is how you're treating me?"

Ross's lips purse together in a sharp line. "It's because of that dedication that you aren't being arrested."

"Arrested?" I scoff. "There's nothing to arrest me for because I didn't do this!"

Ross nods to the two people behind him, and they approach me like they would a rabid cat.

"Unbelievable. I can see myself out."

Stalking out of the room, I don't look back before heading to my office and grabbing my bag and jacket.

My dignity is somewhere back in that conference room.

Investigation? Charges? Arrested?

None of it makes any sense.

The two men flank my side as they escort me out of the office. Curious eyes cast their gazes toward me as I'm led toward the elevators and down to the lobby.

"Miss Stewart, we'll need your access badge."

"I didn't do this," I tell the man standing in front of me as I pull out my badge and slap it into his waiting hand. "This is a mistake."

He doesn't say anything as he heads back up the elevator.

A torrent of emotions is swelling up inside of me. Anger. Frustration. Fear. Sadness. I have no idea what is happening, and I've just been kicked out of the only job I've ever known.

Staring up at the sleek glass building, I can't help but wonder what in the fuck just happened.

Instead of being promoted, I'll be lucky if criminal charges aren't filed against me.

I repeat…what the fuck?

Chapter Two

KIRBY

It feels like a dump truck has run over me. Every muscle in my body is aching—and *not* in a good way. My mouth feels like sandpaper and tastes like the same dump truck that barreled into me.

"Ugh."

I flip onto my back and stare up at the ceiling of my childhood bedroom. Maybe doing all of those shots last night wasn't the best idea.

When I texted Joanne about what happened, she met me at the bar down the street and spent the rest of the day getting absolutely blitzed with me.

Was it the best decision? No. But it was the only thing that could keep me from focusing on the colossal shit storm my life has become.

"Time to wake up."

Light shines into the room and I groan, pulling the comforter up and over my head. "Ugh. Mom!"

"C'mon, Kirb." She yanks the blanket down off me and peers at me with a knowing look. "Lying in bed all day isn't going to fix your problems."

"And getting out of it won't either."

Mom props her fists on her hips and pins me with a motherly stare. "If you wanted to lie in bed all day, you'd have gone to your place rather than calling me to come get you."

"A decision I'm regretting by the minute."

"Should've called a rideshare!" she calls out as she leaves my room. "Breakfast will be ready when you're downstairs."

Okay, this is why I called her. Because as shitty as I'm feeling, I knew she would be there to help pick up the pieces.

Just like she's been doing since the day she brought me home from the hospital.

Heading into the en suite bathroom, a glance in the mirror shows me my red, curly hair is a tangled mess on top of my head. My green eyes are red rimmed from all the drinking.

Dragging a comb through my hair as best I can, I pile it into a messy bun on the top of my head and brush my teeth. The old band T-shirt and sweats I slept in will make do for breakfast.

It's not like I have to dress to impress anyone today.

The sick feeling curdles my stomach. I don't know what I'm going to do if this investigation doesn't prove my innocence. I don't even know where to start to prove it. Because how can you prove something you had no part in doing?

The smells of bacon and eggs waft upstairs, and I quickly find the source of it. Mom is standing in the small kitchen, a plate of my favorite breakfast waiting for me.

"This looks delicious." I breathe in the comforting smells, and it settles the riot of emotions that has taken hold inside me ever since I got the news.

"You're going to eat and then tell me everything that happened."

"Sorry if I worried you." I wince, taking a seat at the island.

"I'm a mother; it's in my nature."

By the time I shovel breakfast down, I'm feeling better. As well as I can be with everything going on.

"That's the gist of it," I tell my mother, giving her the CliffsNotes version of everything that happened.

"Do you think you need an attorney?" she asks. Anger lines her face. "An investigation, my ass. Don't they know you'd never do such a thing?"

Nothing but love floods through me at my mother's words. It makes me feel better to know at least one person is on my side. Joanne could only make me feel somewhat better last night. Telling my mother, the one person in the world that is always going to be on my side, makes it infinitely better. Like maybe I could come out on the right end of this.

"We'll see. Until then, I'm on unpaid leave."

"I guess this is as good a time as any to give you this then."

Mom pulls out an envelope sent to her address.

"What is it?"

Running a finger under the flap, I pull out a thick, folded-up stack of paper.

NOTICE TO HEIRS
Mrs. Elizabeth Taggert

To the heirs and devisees of the above named Estate.
This is formal notice that Elizabeth Anne Taggert, the decedent, died on the thirteenth of July, and you have or may have an interest in the Thistle Hill Lodge located in Loch Ness, Scotland.

The following individual at the following address has been appointed as the administrator of the Estate:
Lee & Travers Law Firm
485 87th Ave
Los Angeles, CA 90751

All documents, pleadings, and information relating to the Estate are on file in the Los Angeles County Courthouse.

I stop reading and look over my shoulder at my mom. "What in the world is this?"

Mom grabs the letter from me and flips through the packet of information. "It looks like this might be your grandmother. Well, biological grandmother."

"How did she find me?"

It's never been a secret that I was adopted. My mom fostered children because she couldn't have biological children of her own. When she got a call that a young mother surrendered her child at the hospital, she came to get me that night, and I've been with her ever since.

"I don't know, sweetheart." Mom wraps her arm around my shoulders. "There's a number here. Why don't you contact them for more information? I don't know what this means."

"She's from Scotland?"

My head is pounding. Too much alcohol from the night before is making it hard to think. I've inherited a house in Scotland? There's no way that's right.

"It looks like it."

There's pictures of an old house, sitting high atop a hill, in the mass of paperwork that Mom is flipping through.

"And what, it's just mine?"

"Call the number. Get more information. See what all of this is about."

I know nothing about my birth parents. After I was dropped off at the hospital and placed with my mom, she adopted me since my birth mother terminated her rights. Last we heard, she passed away, but I never learned anything else about her.

The only family I've ever had is my mom and her parents, although they've long since passed away.

It's always been the two of us, so to find out that I had another relative who knew about me is shocking. I had no idea that this person was out there. Not that I had any reason to go looking, but it could have given me more insight as to where I came from.

"Should I call them now?"

Mom nods, grabbing her coffee and heading out onto the porch. "I'll be outside if you need anything."

"Thanks, Mom."

Grabbing my cell phone from my purse, I head into the cozy living room and drop down into the recliner. Pictures of me growing up cover the walls. I never wanted for anything. My mom gave me the best life possible.

Trips to amusement parks. Weekends spent at the beach. School vacations spent at national parks. I couldn't imagine a better life than the one I got.

"Lee & Travers. How may I assist you?"

The voice on the other end of the call disrupts my thoughts.

"Hi. My name is Kirby Stewart, and I received a notice regarding an estate?" I ask the person on the other end of the line.

"Ahh, yes. Mr. Travers has been expecting your call. One moment."

Jazz music filters through the line as I'm transferred.

"Miss Stewart. How are you?" A loud, booming voice comes over the phone. It has me pulling the phone away from my ear it's so loud.

"Umm, I'm good. I'm calling about the letter I received."

"Yes, yes. We are working with the estate of Mrs. Taggert and her attorneys in Scotland to ensure the house gets to her heir. Which is you."

"But…how?" I press the heel of my hand into my eye to try and stave off the headache that's threatening to overwhelm me. "I don't even know this person."

"Mrs. Taggert used investigators to track you down," he tells me, matter-of-factly.

"Why did she never contact me then?"

Why would someone go through the trouble of trying to find me and then not reach out?

"From what I can tell, she wasn't in the best of health. You are her only heir, and she wanted to make sure her assets were in order before she passed."

"Which is this lodge?" I ask.

"Correct. It is yours free and clear."

"That's it?"

"That's it."

A lodge in Scotland. The last twenty-four hours have been a whirlwind. From thinking I was getting promoted to being investigated to discovering a long-lost relative to now owning a house in Scotland.

"We'll need you to come in and sign some title paperwork so we can get everything in your name, but because the property doesn't have any liens, you will own it with the few strokes of a pen."

A property in Scotland.

I guess there's worse things to own.

Chapter Three

CALLUM

"Time to get yer arse out of bed."

"Mum," I groan.

"I don't care if ye were getting pished until the wee hours. Time to get movin'."

Grabbing my pillow, I pull it over my head, trying to block out the unwelcome morning light. Having had one too many drinks last night, the last thing I want to do is get out of bed.

"Ye'll be sorry if ye don't get up, Callum!" Mum calls as she walks out of my tiny bedroom.

"Give me a minute!" I shout after her.

"Ye've had hours of them."

"Why did I come back home?" I mutter to myself.

Staring at the hard ceiling of my childhood bedroom, it's hard to believe my life has come to this. Not even a few months ago, I was living my best life in the city. Everyone wanted a piece of me. I was at the top of my field.

And now?

Now, I'm back home, living with me Mum like a wee'un who cannae get his life together.

Life sucks right now.

I scrub a hand down my face, through my beard that has grown in thick. Maybe if I cared more, I'd shave it, but I don't have it in me.

And that's when it happens. Ice-cold water crashes down all over me.

"Mum! What the fuck?!"

Scrambling to get out of the bed that is too small for my massive frame, I fall straight to the ground. The blankets are a tangled mess at my feet.

"I told ye, time to get movin'."

I wipe the dripping water from my eyes. "And that's how you decided to do it?"

Mum gives me a smile that, had this been done to anyone else but me, I would return. "Bet ye aren't feeling so tipsy anymore."

"Fuck me."

Mum pierces me with a fierce stare. "Five minutes, Callum. Let's go."

"It'll take me at least ten now!" I call after her, but it's no use.

When she says five minutes, she means it. Heading into the small bathroom, I duck down so I don't slam my head on the doorframe.

I've made that mistake one too many times.

I drag a brush through the mess of brown hair and pull the long locks into a tight bun on top of my head. It's about all I can muster right now, because as much as I hate to admit it, Mum was right.

I stayed out way too late with the lads.

When I've got nothing going for me, it's easy to get swept up in not having anything to do.

Another pint? Why the fuck not?

"Would you look at that?" Mum says by way of

greeting when I finally make it downstairs to the tiny kitchen. "You can wake up before noon."

Would it be rude to flip my mum off? Because that's where I am right now.

"I'll break yer fingers off if you try it."

"What?" I grab a mug from the counter and pour myself a cup of coffee.

"I know what ye're thinking, Callum. I've raised ye, so I know ye're thinking some unkind things right now."

I snort around the hot brew I just poured. Of course she knows this. What is it with mothers being all-knowing? It's weird.

I drop down into the chair in the breakfast nook that sits off the small space. Rain patters against the window that sits above the sink. All sorts of ingredients for something she's baking line the small counter next to it.

"Now, Fiona needs yer help today down at the fields to set up for the games. And ol' man Thomas needs help at the hardware store today. Think ye can manage that?"

I lean back in the chair, resting its weight on two legs. The creak it gives is ominous. I'm not sure if it can hold my weight.

I cannae complain. There's worse places I could have landed. Mum wouldn't let me wallow in misery. Except… the minute I came home, I became the person to help everyone else out whenever they need it. The town handyman if you will.

Even though I widnae consider myself handy at all. Nothing like learning on the fly.

"I told Fiona ye'd be down there by half ten. Don't dawdle." Mum grabs the cup from my hand and dumps it into a travel mug. "Get those boots and get going."

"Christ, Mum. I cannae even finish me coffee?" I gripe.

"Maybe if ye didnae sleep so late, you would." She hands me a wrapped up sandwich in a towel. "Breakfast for ye. Now, dinnae be late. Shoo."

Not having more than a minute to stuff my feet into my boots, I'm shoved out the door, breakfast and coffee in hand.

Aberlach is a small town, nestled right on the banks of Loch Ness. The hills surrounding the loch are filled with manor houses turned into inns to host the heaps of people that come visit every year hoping to spot our infamous Nessie.

I shouldn't be so put off by it. They keep our small town afloat. But on days like today, where the weather is pissing rain, they stay hidden away. Like they're going to melt.

A handful of villagers wave at me as I head down the hill toward the large, open field where the town's fall Highland games will be held in a few weeks.

Something else I've been dragged into doing. Mum said something about people wanting to see me in a kilt.

Anything other than an aye and Mum would've flayed me with a spoon. And now, I'm being sent to help set the games up.

An older, squat woman with bejeweled glasses is waving like a bampot at me. Ol' Fiona has been around longer than I can remember.

"If it isn't Callum MacRae as I live and breathe."

Fiona pulls me down into a smothering hug. She smells like whisky and honey.

"Fiona. How are ye?" I ask, wrapping an arm around her. As much as the old bat drives me crazy, she has a heart of gold and would do anything for anyone.

Maybe that's why I agreed to me mum and her whims.

"Callum. How good to see ye. It's been too long."

Fiona squeezes my cheek. "Ye look too skinny. Have ye been eating enough?"

I pull back from her arms and look down my body. The very last thing anyone would use to describe me is skinny. I have more muscles than I know what to do with most days.

"I'm eating just fine."

She pats my stomach. My very hard, six-pack abs stomach. "Yer mum needs to get more meat on these bones."

I smile down at her. "I'll be sure to tell her you said that."

Fiona eyes me through her glasses. "I don't think ye will, so I'll be sure to give her my new black pudding recipe."

"Mum said you needed help?" I steer the conversation away from anything resembling black pudding. It's my least favorite thing, and there aren't enough hours in the day to listen to Fiona prattle on about her famous recipes that she serves at her bakery.

"All of these programs need to be moved to the shed. Came to town hall. Can ye believe it?"

I laugh, grabbing the first two boxes with ease. "Not a problem."

"I hear Miriam is keeping you busy?"

"Aye. Mum winnae let me sit around on my arse." Not that being kept busy is a bad thing.

"Too busy to come see me?"

I wince. Leave it to these old women to guilt you for not seeing them.

"Sorry. It's been a long few weeks."

"Tsk. Terrible what happened."

There's not much I can do but nod. Because what else can I say? Having my nan die and my wife run off with my accountant *and* all my money in the same week isn't the easiest thing to talk about.

"I hear Mary is single now." Fiona walks along next to me across the field. The rain has lightened, but it's created mud pits throughout the field.

Don't take the bait, Callum. Don't take the bait.

"Moved back home from the city after dumping that loser boyfriend of hers. Looking for someone more stable."

She's eyeing me up and down with a knowing gaze.

"Loser boyfriend?"

Christ, why am I engaging? This is the reason I didnae want to move back home. Aberlach is filled with busybodies. Since the minute I arrived back home, all of Mum's friends have been trying to pawn me off on any unsuspecting single woman in town.

Never mind that my divorce was only finalized a few days ago. Hence going out and getting pished off my arse with the lads.

She squeezes my bicep. "He disnae come from good stock like you."

"Maybe give the poor lass some breathing room, yeah?" I tell her. "She probably disnae want to be set up."

Fiona shakes her head at me. "Oh no, Callum. When I told her ye were back in town, she said aye."

Fuck me. This is the last thing I need. In this place, there's no room to lick your wounds. Mum keeps me so busy that I'm out the door first thing in the morning and not home until I'm falling into bed at night.

"I appreciate ye, Fiona, but I'm not interested."

"Of course ye are! Who widnae want to be with someone like her?"

Setting the box down, I make a show of starting to go through it. This is the very last thing I want. The ink is barely dry on my divorce papers and she thinks I'm someone that Mary wants to be with?

Mary… I'm trying to rack my brain to remember her from school, but I cannae.

I huvnae been the best son these last few years. As soon as I graduated from uni, I moved to Edinburgh and have only made it back home a few times each year. It was a short drive, but I always had an excuse.

One excuse too many is exactly the reason I'm here now. In this situation that I don't know how to get myself out of.

"Fine, ignore me, Callum MacRae, but yer mum will hear about this."

Fuck me.

I'm not sure which is worse. Trying to play off someone being interested in me, ignoring the ol' bat that is setting me up, or her telling on me to me mum.

Just what I wanted. Mum handing my arse to me.

Life really does suck.

Chapter Four

KIRBY

"I'm sorry, how much?"

"Two hundred quid."

Quid, quid, quid. I'm racking my brain as I stare at the person across the car rental counter. My brain is sluggish. After spending a hellacious fourteen hours stuck in middle seats—on the best flights I could find that didn't cost a small fortune—on my multiple connections to get here, I'm exhausted. I don't know what time zone I'm in, let alone what day it is.

Trying to figure out how much I'm paying for an open-ended car rental? No chance of that happening.

"Okay." I hand over my credit card and license without trying to make heads or tails of it.

"Ye know how ta drive here?" the man across the counter asks.

"Sure."

"Watch out for the one-lane roads. Ye're heading to the Highlands, aye? Not like yer roads back home."

"One-lane roads. Got it."

He eyes me up and down, looking at me like I don't, in fact, got it.

It's the truth. I'm about as far from having it together as I possibly could be. After meeting with the attorneys of my grandmother's estate, things moved quickly. With no other heirs, the title work went through easily.

Now, two weeks later, I'm a ball of exhaustion, standing in the Edinburgh airport on my way to a house I now own.

Not exactly where I saw myself. I assumed I'd be mixing with the VPs of our company, as the newly crowned head of my department.

When I told Joanne what I was doing, she encouraged me to go. To lie low while the buzz died down around the investigation. With no work to do, why not come and see this house that I'm the owner of?

Besides, it's Scotland. Who wouldn't want to come here?

"Aye. Here ye go, bonny lass." He gives me a toothy grin while passing over the keys. "It's not much, but should get ye where ye need to go."

"Thanks."

Swiping the keys from him, I head out to the appropriate stall and stop dead in my tracks.

The car in front of me doesn't look bigger than a matchbox. Can it even hold the giant suitcase I'm wheeling behind me? The blue paint at least looks like it's in good condition, but there are only two doors. I have no idea how I'm going to finagle my bag inside.

"You can do this, Kirby. You've done harder things."

It's a mantra I have no doubt I'm going to be telling myself a lot over these next few weeks.

When the attorney told me that the house needed some work, I figured I could spruce the place up and turn around and sell it. I've wielded many a paint roller in my life. A fresh coat of paint and then hopefully making some money off the sale? Not the worst way to spend a few weeks while I wait out the investigation. Besides, my life is back in LA. Not Scotland.

Stuffing my bags into the back of the car as best I can, I head toward the left side of the car. The minute I sit down, I realize my mistake.

The steering wheel is on the other side of the car.

Fuck. Am I really equipped to be driving on the other side of the road with little to no sleep in the last twenty-four hours?

I stifle my scream of frustration as I get out of the car and head toward the correct side. The one *with* the steering wheel.

Traffic isn't nearly as heavy as at home as I cautiously pull out into the first traffic circle. Being outside the city, it's not as bad as I thought. The roads are wet as rain pelts the windshield.

"See? You can do this, Kirby," I tell myself. "Easy. You've done harder things than this."

But the farther I get into the country, the faster night seems to fall. It's not late, but with the dark clouds, it's getting harder and harder to see.

Maybe I should pull off and find a hotel for the night. Do this drive with a clear head in the morning. Except... there's nothing.

No hotels. No motels. Nothing.

"Crap."

My plan is blown to hell because there is nothing but darkness as far as the eye can see.

In the hour that I've been on the road, I haven't found any place to stop. So when my exit comes up, I breathe a sigh of relief.

Glancing down at the GPS on my phone, it looks like it's another forty-five minutes to the inn.

I give myself the same pep talk to keep going. I'm not one to back down from hard situations. When the going gets tough, I thrive. I'm made for situations like this.

The lane narrows as I amble along the country road. Trees hang over the road, making it even more ominous. I looked up the small town I would be staying in, and it looked picturesque.

Now if only I can make it there.

A set of blinding headlights pull out in front of me, and my hands squeeze the steering wheel. Whoever this is seems to be making no move to stop. They're barreling toward me.

"Oh my God, oh my God, oh my God!" I scream, closing my eyes and swerving out of the way. The car bumps along and comes to a sudden stop.

Looking back, the tractor driver is muddling along and I'm sitting in a bank on the side of the road.

Holy shit. Throwing open the car door, I'm in a small pullout in the road with a sign posted that reads "passing place."

Huh. Looking up and down the road as far as I can see, I realize this must be what the agent at the airport was telling me about.

"One lane? What the fuck?" I murmur, taking a deep breath to quell my anxious nerves.

Optimistic pep talks have gone to hell now. If this is what Scotland is going to be like, I don't know if I'm cut out for it.

Until a loud moo cuts through the silence next to me.

"Holy shit!" I scream, jumping and landing with a thud in a pool of mud.

The cause of the screaming-moo comes into view in

the headlights of my car. The burnt-orange cow with horns stares at me from beyond the barbed wire fence.

If my heart wasn't threatening to beat out of my chest, I'd coo over how cute this guy is. "You just had to scare me tonight of all nights."

His brown eyes stare at me, as he continues chomping on whatever grass is in his mouth. Is this what my life has come to? Talking to cows on the side of a dark road in the middle of nowhere Scotland?

I take a deep breath, and the cool, Scottish air helps settle all the nerves inside me. This is about as far from the hustle and bustle of LA as you can get.

"You can do this, Kirby." I give myself yet *another* pep talk. "Get your ass back into that car and find your new house."

By the time I muster up the energy to get back on the road—wiping off as much mud as I can before getting into my tiny rental—I'm pulling into town and ready to crash. I don't care where—my body is ready to collapse in on itself.

Gas streetlamps light up the town. Old brick buildings line either side of the road. Short stone walls run alongside the sidewalks. By the time my eyes are done taking everything in, I'm on the opposite end of town.

Blink and you miss it. An old beat-up sign sits at the curve in the road.

Thistle Hill Lodge.

Breathing out a sigh of relief, at least I've found where I need to go. There are no streetlights as I turn my car onto a windy, curvy road that leads up the side of a hill. Coming to a fork in the road, I follow a second sign nailed into a tree that points me in the direction I need to go.

A potholed road leads the way with scraggly trees on the sides. When I spot a gated entryway, both metal gates are falling off their hinges. There's a small pullout where I park the car and get out.

"What the hell?"

Slamming the car door behind me, I take in the shabby house in front of me. The photos I saw displayed a house that was in better shape than this. The only thing that looks like it's in decent shape is the sloping front lawn. I can only imagine what the views look like when it's not shrouded in darkness.

The front door of the lodge is flanked by two sets of windows with shutters barely hanging on. This entire side of the house looks like it could do with a good scrubbing.

This is what I signed up for?

The old iron key takes some finagling to get into the lock, but once it slides in, the door opens with little effort. As tired as I am, I'm a problem solver. I'm already making a mental list of everything that needs to be done.

So much for a few cans of paint and I'm done.

Turning on the flashlight on my phone, I find a lone light switch, and it flickers to life. Even if it's faint.

Cobwebs hang from every available surface, and what must be years of dust covers the place. Old wallpaper is peeling from the walls.

"What have you gotten yourself into, Kirb?" I ask myself as I head into a room with windows lining one wall. A bar cuts through the room, and old kitchen appliances take up one wall. The windows are grimy with the reflection of my flashlight reflecting back at me.

Continuing my tour of the house, I find a small bathroom off to the right of the kitchen before the room opens into what appears to be a sitting room.

I flip on the light to the bathroom, and it at least seems to cast more light into the house. The mirror hanging above the sink is cracked. The water in the toilet? As brown as the filth on the walls in here.

"Does this even work?"

Pushing on the handle, I watch as the water gurgles before a loud gush erupts from the bowl.

"Holy shit!"

Water rains down over me as I struggle to wipe it out of my eyes to turn the water off. I could cry. Everything about this day has been absolutely shit and I don't know how to make it better.

"Who the fuck are ye?" comes a loud booming voice from behind me.

"Holy shit!"

I jump, crashing down on the uneven floor and flopping over the ancient ceramic bowl. Scotland has apparently reduced my vocabulary to only these two words. What else can I say other than that when I'm covered in toilet water and a stranger is standing before me?

And that's when my humiliation peaks for the day. Because standing in the doorframe is the burliest, and quite possibly sexiest, man I've ever met.

"Holy shit!"

Chapter Five

CALLUM

What in the ever-living hell is going on now?

It's been another day that winnae seem to end. By the time I finally got home and settled in with a pint then glanced over to see the light flip on at the old manor house, I'd had enough.

No one has been at this house in years. Or so me mum tells me.

It might not have been one of my better ideas to come over here and see what is going on. But what else do I have to do?

Now, there's a bampot in the bathroom covered in toilet water. A sexy redhead who looks mad with all that wild hair, but a bampot, nonetheless.

"What in the fuck are ye doin' here?" I ask her.

Hazel eyes stare back at me like I've lost my mind. Those green pools are raking over me, taking in my frame that barely fits in the doorway. It's like she disnae know what to make of me, this stranger just showing up out of the blue.

Except, she did the exact same thing.

"You cannae just waltz in here like ye own the place."

That has her eyes clearing, as she wipes water from her cheeks. "I do own the place."

I snort a laugh. "Sorry, lass. This place here is owned by Lizzie. Try again."

"Lizzie?" she asks.

Crossing my arms, I dinnae respond and stare her down. I'm not going to let this fiery bonny lass try and get one over on me. She's the one that's where she isnae supposed to be.

Hell, I'm surprised she was able to get in the front door.

"This Lizzie, you say, she owned the place?" the woman asks me. She approaches me with all the grace of a bull in a china shop. Maybe this is why she's covered in toilet water.

"Aye."

Her brows pinch together, studying me. If she thinks she's going to intimidate me into backing down, she's got another think coming.

I didnae become Scotland's youngest billionaire by cowering to others.

No matter how sexy they are.

"Would you believe she's my grandmother?"

This gets another laugh out of me. "Lizzie? She didnae have any grandkids."

If there's one thing I know about ol' Lizzie Taggert it's that she never had grandkids. Always wanted them, so she took everyone in town under her wing. Treats, a card on your birthday, a dinner when you were down.

Lizzie was there for everyone. So when she passed, the town took it hard. And now this lass shows up expecting me to believe her?

I'll believe a lot of fucking wild things, but not this.

"She does. Well, did. And I'm her."

She takes another step towards me. I dinnae have a clue who she is, but I like that she's not taking my shit.

A smile crooks at the corner of my mouth. "Prove it."

"What, you want me to share a DNA test with you? I have the deed to this place from my attorney. I was her only living relative."

"Sassy."

She rolls those green eyes at me and reaches into the front pocket of her jeans, pulling out an old, worn metal key.

"Does this prove anything? How else would I have this?"

My eyes flit to the tarnished key. I know it's the key to this place, because we have a matching one. Since Lizzie died, Mum has been looking after the grounds of the old place. With the lodge being on the same road, it was easy for her. Not that the house is anything to go by, but from what I'm told, it used to be quite the place to be back in the day.

"What's yer name?" I ask her.

"Kirby."

"Kirby?"

"Repeating it isn't going to change it." Kirby matches my stance, standing only an inch from me. She's a good head shorter than I am. I could rest my elbows comfortably on her shoulders and then some. But that red hair of hers, frizzing out every which way, makes her look taller.

I wonder how it would look wrapped around my fist as I'm fucking her.

Shit. That is not a thought I need to be having right now. Not about this random stranger who just showed up here.

"And you decided to show up now?"

"Are you always like this?" Kirby asks. "It's not like I knew about her."

"Why not?"

Red flames up her pretty cheeks. The fieriness is coming out. It only makes me wonder how she'd be in bed. Again, not thoughts I need to be having.

But it's been a right minute since I've been with anyone.

"I'm sorry, but do I need to give you my life story in order to prove I'm related to a woman I never met? What are you, the head of the town welcoming committee? Because if so, I might need to have a word with them," Kirby scoffs.

"Not the welcoming committee. Just making sure that random women dinnae come bursting into places they dinnae belong."

Kirby presses up onto her tiptoes, jutting her chin out towards me. "I assure you, I belong. Would you like to see the deed?"

If I say aye, she will probably rip my head off. Is it bad I want to see that reaction out of her?

"I believe you…for now."

"How gracious of you." She places her hand on the center of my chest, and it's all I can do to ignore the heat that fills the empty cavity there. "Now, if you don't mind, would you get out of my way?"

I don't budge. Something about this woman has me rooted to the spot. It's been four long months. Days filled with work around town to keep the intrusive thoughts at bay of how my life went up in smoke.

Now, for the first time, it's the furthest thing from my mind. Do I want to get into a pissing match with her? I certainly widnae mind it.

"Where do ye have to go?"

"Anywhere where you're not." She makes a move to duck around me, but I throw my hand to the side of the doorframe, enclosing her in. "God. Why are you so infuriating? I don't even know your name, and I want to scream it because you're driving me crazy!"

Leaning down, my mouth is a breath away from her ear. She stills. I don't miss the small inhale she takes. "It's Callum. And I assure you, I'd have you screaming my name in a much more pleasurable way."

Kirby shifts, ever so slightly, so her eyes are locked on mine. I could move not more than a millimeter and I'd be kissing her. Fuck, why is that thought so intriguing?

"I assure *you*, Callum, that screaming your name as I throw you out of my house is very pleasurable for me."

I've let down my defences enough that when she pushes me back, I stumble out of the doorway and into the opposite wall. The look of satisfaction on her face tells me she knows she got one up on me.

"Now, if you'll excuse me, I have a house to assess." Apparently not one to leave well enough alone, she peeks over her shoulder at me. "And no staring at my ass when I walk away."

"Widnae dream of it."

Kirby spins, walking backwards into the lounge. Or at least what I remember of this place being the lounge. It's been a good few years since I've stepped back inside it.

"That's the only place you'll see me again, Callum. In your dreams."

She saunters away without another word.

Oh, I will, lass. I fucking will.

Chapter Six

KIRBY

It feels like someone is watching me. I hope that beast of a man didn't decide to break in again. Not that I'd mind seeing him again. But it feels like there is someone with me in this room.

After stalking away from my late-night visitor, I found the one room in this place with a bed that looked like it was suitable for sleeping.

Light creeps in through the moth-eaten curtains. I can see the gray skies and rain pelting the windows.

Sitting up, all I can see is the sloping front lawn that trails alongside the main drive. A smaller cottage sits nearby, just down the road. It looks well kept. It's about the only thing that is.

Fishing a hoodie out of my bag, I find my tennis shoes and head out of the bedroom to see the rest of the house again. In the daylight, it looks only slightly better than it did last night.

I don't have the first clue on how to fix up a house, but that's what the Internet is for, right? Shipping manifests and port fees are something I can deal with in my sleep, but since I'm currently under investigation, I can't do much of anything. Since I don't know who is setting me up, I may as well think about something else because I have no idea how to prove it wasn't me.

I guess fixing up a house is the only thing I should focus on until my name gets cleared.

Making a mental list of everything I might need, I push open the back door to take in the small, fenced-in yard.

A garden lines the low stone wall, and a tiny outbuilding sits farther back. Curiosity gets the better of me, so I pull the hood of my sweatshirt up and head toward it.

I have no idea what this is. I've lived in LA my entire life. Napa is as far away from the city as I've been, and I've taken a few short trips to Mexico, but that's not all that far from home. I was made for the hustle and bustle of life there.

But with nothing going for me back home, I resign myself to exploring my new surroundings. I pull open the wood door, and a rustle of feathers attacks me.

"Ahh!" I shriek as a rooster explodes out of what I now know is a chicken coop. Cartwheeling my arms, I try to catch myself, but with a squelch, end up in the mud. "Fuck me!"

"Now is that any way to talk with a poorly cock around?"

That voice. God, that infuriating voice coming from a mouth that I can't decide if I want to punch or kiss.

Definitely punch. I think. I'm too jet-lagged to think straight.

Opening one eye, I'm met with a pair of legs. And a skirt. Or rather, a kilt?

"Like the view, bonny lass?"

"Cal! Help the poor lass up!" Another voice enters the fray. This time, an older woman's voice.

Could life get any more embarrassing for me here? How many people are going to witness my humiliation?

I'm going to need to invest in a good washer if I'm going to keep landing in the mud at every turn.

The first time I met this man, I was covered in toilet water. Now? Now I'm staring up his kilt. It's like I left all my good sense back home the minute I stepped onto that plane.

Or maybe work stole all my dignity when I was escorted out for stealing money. *Supposedly* stealing money. Because why the hell would I need to steal when I was a saver to start with?

"Ye alright?"

The way the word comes off his tongue as he hoists me up does funny things to my insides. Mud clings to me.

"Fine. Never better."

Callum doesn't drop my hand, just squeezes it a little tighter. What is this man doing to me? Everything inside me is all twisted up.

Down is up and up is down.

Black is white and white is black.

Nothing makes sense to me.

This guy is so far from my type, I wouldn't even know what to do with myself. So why, then, do I want to climb him like a tree?

"I'm sorry about me bairn here. I raised him to have better manners than that."

I can't help the laugh that escapes or the way that Callum looks chagrined. So this is his mother.

"I hear ye're Lizzie's granddaughter."

I stare at Callum. In the daylight, he looks even more imposing. His biceps are thick—hell, probably as thick as my head. I didn't get a good look up his kilt—only enough to see strong legs covered in dark hair. "Cal didn't say much about ye."

"Hi." I brush my hands off on my jeans. Not that it does much since I'm covered in mud, but I thrust my hand out to her anyway. "Kirby."

"Miriam. And ye met this oaf."

"Mum," he grumbles.

Ignoring the man behind her, I give her a warm smile. Callum is the spitting image of her. They have the same blue eyes. Same dark hair, although Miriam's has more white laced through it. She's taller than I am, but not as tall as the man behind her.

"I guess we're neighbors?"

"Aye." She reaches behind her, patting Callum's thick, veined forearm. Something I should *not* be noticing. "When did ye arrive?"

"Last night."

Miriam nods. "I'm sorry to hear about yer nan. Lizzie was a wonderful woman."

"I wish I had known her."

Even if I only could have known her for a little while, I might have learned more about my birth mom. Not that I ever wanted for anything in my life. I had the best mother I ever could have asked for. It didn't mean I didn't want to know more about where I came from. That was always a mystery to me.

"And ye have her inn now? What are ye going to do with it?" Miriam looks behind me at the dilapidated building.

It's nothing to write home about. Shutters hanging off the siding. Windows with cracked glass. It looks like it could use a good hosing down.

"I'm going to fix it up." I instill more confidence in my voice than I feel. *Fake it 'til you make it, right?*

Miriam's bright blue eyes light up. "I have an idea!"

"Oh no," Callum mutters behind her.

I have a feeling I know where this is going, but I don't say anything.

"Cal can help! Right?" She spins on her heel to look at him. "He's right handy with a hammer. He'll help ye get this place up and running in no time."

Miriam is way too gleeful for this early in the morning. Especially when I'm covered in mud. Hopefully *only* mud. And nothing else I might find in the chicken coop.

"I thought I was supposed to be helping Fiona set up for the games?" he asks. His face is contorted like he was just told that he has to get a tooth pulled.

I'm not looking forward to this either, Callum. A broody Scot in my space? One who is already driving me up the wall? Yeah, this won't work.

"I'll help her. Yer skills can help welcome our Kirby into Aberlach."

I don't miss the way she says *our* Kirby. Like even though I just got to town, I'm one of them. Almost by default since Lizzie was my grandma.

"But—"

Miriam interrupts Callum. "No buts. I raised ye to help people in need, ye ken?"

Callum doesn't say anything, just grinds that perfect jaw of his, covered with a thick beard.

"I don't want to take him away from his important work."

Miriam waves me off. "Nonsense, lass. That's why Callum is here."

"Here?"

"He—"

"Mum!" This time, Callum's interruption is met with silence. I have a feeling whatever his mom was about to say, he doesn't want shared.

Alright then.

"Ye arse," she chides him. "I'll have Cal here tomorrow, bright and early."

"How early?" I ask. I could use another twenty-four hours of sleep.

"When the roosters crow."

Miriam pats my cheek and is off down the road, Callum on her heels.

He turns back, looking at me then the house.

I have no idea what the two of us just got ourselves into, but I'm not looking forward to it.

Because the last thing I need in my life is a broody Scot that I can't get a read on.

Chapter Seven

CALLUM

"I cannae believe ye volunteered me for this, Mum."

Mum swats me with the tea towel in her hand. "The poor lass has no one to help her. Dinnae be a numpty and show her yer skills."

"My skills?" I quirk a brow at her as I glug down the rest of my coffee. "Mum, I've never fixed up a house before."

She waves me off like this isn't a problem at all. "Ye'll learn."

Forget the fact that I do menial jobs around town, but a whole house? I dinnae know how in the fuck I'm going to make this work.

"Now, get going, Cal. I dinnae want to see ye here before dinner."

"Christ, Mum. Can I at least finish my coffee?"

She grabs the empty mug from my hand. "And ye're done. Now, get going."

Shoving my feet into my boots, I grab my jacket to ward off the cool morning air and head up the road for the manor house.

It's in a right state. I have no idea why Mum thinks I'm the right man for this job. I never worked with my hands before moving back home. Working in tech, I didnae need to. Building apps and software for companies was where I excelled.

Helping Kirby fix up this house?

That remains to be seen.

"Are you just going to stand there, or are you going to help?" Kirby calls out from the front door.

Stalking up to her, I cannae help it as my eyes take her in. All that red hair of hers is piled on top of her head. Her face is bare of all makeup. Freckles dance across the bridge of her nose. An old sweatshirt is stretched tight across her chest. And those green eyes of hers? They are returning the favor—casting an easy perusal of me as I stop in front of her.

"Seeing what I got myself into."

"More like what your mom roped you into."

She's not wrong. But I cannae tell her she would hand my arse to me if I backed out now. Mum is much scarier than anything this woman can dole out to me.

"Where are we going to start?" I ask, stepping up onto the front stoop. It's chipped and falling apart, just like the rest of the house.

Kirby heads back into the house and I follow her. "I figured we could start in the…living room? Parlor?"

"Lounge. I didnae realize this place was so run-down." The other night, darkness cloaked most of the inside from view. Now, in the harsh light of day, I dinnae know what Mum signed me up for. "Are you sure you know what you're getting yourself into?" I ask. "This looks like a lot more work than I bargained for."

Tarps are draped over the furniture. A small box of

tools sits in the middle of the room. The windows are thrown open, letting in the cool morning air.

"What,"—Kirby steps toward me, standing chest to chest with me—"afraid of a little challenge?"

I dinnae know what it is about this woman, but she's egging me on. If she thinks she's going to get me to back down, she's going to be surprised. "You wish, lass."

She studies me before answering. "Good. Then let's get started."

"I want to knock down this wall," Kirby tells me, pointing to a short half wall that divides the room in a weird way. "I think it'll open things up."

"And how are we taking it down?"

Kirby points to the center of the room. "Sledgehammer."

"Did you ask anyone before you decided to do this?"

She shrugs a slim shoulder. "The man down at the hardware store said it would do just fine."

Of course Thomas said that. I can only imagine his reaction when Kirby waltzed into his store and asked for things to what…tear down a house?

One look at this woman tells me I don't think she's ever done a lick of manual labor in her life. And she thinks she can fix this entire house?

I'm skeptical at best.

"You think I can't do this."

Walking to the center of the room, I pick up the hammer and hold it out to her. "Let's see ye do it then."

A flush washes over her cheeks, like I pissed her off. Maybe that'll be her motivation to prove me wrong.

Kirby takes the hammer from my hand, grabs a pair of safety glasses, and marches over to the wall. I can feel her determination from here.

Hefting the weight of the tool in her hands, she bends

down and sets her pose. Pulling it back, she slams the metal head into the wall.

"Shit!" Kirby shouts, as the wall explodes. Plaster dust settles over the two of us.

"Have ye ever done this before?"

Kirby swipes at a piece of dirt on her face. It does nothing except move the dust around. "If you think you know better, you do it."

I grab the hammer from her and line myself to take a swing where she made the first strike. It's not as big of a bang, but more wood and plaster come out.

"You're not much better."

After two swings, it looks like we've barely taken a chunk out of the wall. Fuck. If we have to take out more walls than this tiny one, it could take a year given how bad we are.

"Mum volunteered me. This isnae something I know how to do."

Kirby rolls her eyes at me. "Great, so you're useless."

Kirby tries to grab the sledgehammer back from me, but I dinnae let her. Instead, I tug her towards me. "Not quite useless, lass."

Something flickers in those green eyes of hers. "That remains to be seen."

"Careful what you wish for, love." I'm never one to back down.

"You know, I didn't ask for your help."

"You've got it anyway."

"Are you always this argumentative?" Kirby huffs out.

"Are you?" I throw back at her. "You're the one who is insistent on doing this yourself."

"Because I can."

Christ, why is this woman arguing with me such a turn-on? Maybe I'm starved for a woman's attention, so the first one that crosses my path will do.

"Do you ever take help from anyone?"

Kirby pushes a stray strand of dust-caked hair out of her face. "No. I wouldn't have gotten where I did if I asked for help anytime I didn't know what to do."

"And where is here exactly? Because from where I'm standing, you're in the same place as I am."

"You don't know anything about me," Kirby tells me, shoving a finger in the center of my chest. "Don't act like you do."

"I dinnae think I have." I grab her finger and pull her closer.

"Then stop doubting me."

"Take this down and prove me wrong then."

And prove me wrong she does. There is something about a person determined to show me up that I find attractive. I shouldn't, considering that is how I fell for my first wife. My now *ex-wife*.

It's not the best job I've seen, in my limited experience. But in the span of a few minutes, the spitfire of a woman has the half wall down.

"See?" Her chest is heaving from exertion as she drops the head of the sledgehammer to the floor and rests her weight on it. "No big deal."

Is it bad I want to continue to egg her on to see what she can do? Hell, maybe even what she can do in the bedroom. I am definitely taken with this woman.

Shaking off the stupor she's put me in, I examine the remnants of the wall. "Not bad."

"Not bad?" she parrots back at me. "I'd like to see you do the same."

I smile at her. She's a mess, but I cannae help but like it. "I cannae."

"And why not?" She drops the sledgehammer and approaches me. Why are we in a tit for tat with one another?

"Because you already knocked it down."

A sheepish look washes over Kirby's face. "Fine. I'm sure we can find something else for you to prove your skills."

"Aye, lass. That's not a contest I need to get in with you."

"Don't want to get into a dick swinging contest with me?"

I choke around a laugh. "Christ, you cannae say things like that."

"Says who?" She crosses her arms, dust still caked on them.

Cal, shake it off. You dinnae need to be smitten with this woman.

"Did I say I wanted to get into a pissing match with you?"

"You seem to think I can't do it."

I wave a hand to the destruction behind her. "Seems like you did just fine without me."

"Damn straight."

"Now what?" I don't let her win this argument. Just because the wall is down, disnae mean our job is done. A half wall in one room of this house isnae gonna make much difference.

Kirby shakes her head at me. "Can you just let me have this one win?"

I give her one firm nod. "Fine. Ye did a great job, lass."

She rolls her eyes at me. "Don't humor me."

"Christ. I cannae win with you, can I?"

"No one said you needed to help me."

"Back to this again, are we?" I ask her.

I enjoy arguing with her far too much. Something

about it has me coming out of the shell I've shrunk into the last few months. But I'll never admit it to her.

"If you're going to help me, can you do it with less attitude? I've dealt with men with small-dick syndrome before and I hate it."

The gall of this woman. "I assure you, Kirby. That is not what I'm compensating for."

Her green eyes take a long, slow perusal over me. I dinnae stir under her gaze. I welcome it. For the first time in a long time, I feel alive. With my ex-wife, I was just letting life pass me by—even before she ran off on me. It wisnae the healthiest of ways to live. Moving back to Aberlach hasnae been easy either. Just going through the motions isnae the best way.

But now, under Kirby's stare, I'm feeling more like myself than I have in years. The push and pull is something I welcome. I want to poke and prod at her to see how far I can push her.

Will she yell at me? Kiss me? Fuck me?

Things I dinnae need to be thinking, but damn, Kirby is a force to be reckoned with.

"I'd say I know what I'm dealing with, but I don't."

"What are you saying?" I ask.

Approaching me with all the care of a wild animal, Kirby shoves the sledgehammer into my chest.

"If you feel the need to swing your dick, take it elsewhere. I don't need to see it."

"You don't?" I quirk a brow at her.

A slight flush creeps up her cheeks. I can see how much she's focusing on *not* looking down. I hate that this woman is bringing out such a reaction in me.

"No. Keep it in your pants." Pushing me back away from her, Kirby walks by me in a whiff of vanilla and sass. "Now, get it together because we've got more work to do."

Damn. This woman could command me at every turn and I'd willingly follow.

What the hell does that say about me? The last thing I'm gonna let her know is how much she's affecting me.

Fuck, no.

I'm a pro at hiding my emotions. I dinnae need to let this lass know how she's making me feel. No matter how badly I want to act on it.

Damn this woman. If only it were that easy.

Chapter Eight

CALLUM

"Callum. What are ye doing down here?" Fiona says by way of greeting, surprise written all over her face.

"Cannae a man eat?" I rest my hands on the wooden counter of her bakery. The smell of sugar is strong. Sweets and treats of all kinds sit behind the glass displays. The specials of the day are scrawled across the chalkboard that hangs on the bright, yellow-painted wall behind the cappuccino makers.

Fiona looks at her watch in dramatic fashion. "I dinnae think I've seen you down here before noon."

I scrub a hand over the back of my neck. This is the one thing I hated when I moved home. How in your business everyone is.

"I'm meeting Kirby here."

"The new girl?" Fiona leans across the counter, her grey curls bouncing in delight. "What are ye doing with her?"

"Can I order yet?" I ask instead of answering.

"If you tell me what ye're meeting the lass for."

"Not that it's any of yer business, but I'm helping her fix up her house."

"Lizzie's ol' place?"

"That's the one." I grab my wallet from my back pocket. "Coffee and buttery, please."

Fiona rolls her eyes at me and punches in my order. "Alright. I'll bring it over to ye."

"Thanks."

I hand her a twenty-pound note and find a seat along the wall in one of the red metal chairs. Oversized, stuffed red chairs sit under the bay window in the front. I have a feeling Kirby would love sitting there to people watch, but the last thing I want is for the two of us to be on display for the entire town like fish in a bowl.

"Here ye are." Fiona drops off my order. "Let me know if ye need anything else."

"Aye." I nod my thanks and take a long sip of the bitter coffee. Fuck, I needed it.

As annoying as Fiona's comments are, she's not wrong. After my wife ran off with my accountant, I didnae have a lot going for me. Add losing my life savings to the list and it made me not want to get out of bed in the morning.

If it weren't for Mum, I wouldn't be here right now.

Sipping on the hot liquid, I keep my eyes out for the woman that I'm helping. I might not know much about fixing up houses, but I know we need a plan. We cannae just keep taking down walls and hoping for the best.

The bell above the door chimes, and like a whirlwind, the woman waltzes in.

Christ.

Kirby marches right up to the counter, and instead of simply placing her order, has a much longer than necessary conversation with Fiona.

I smirk as I sip my coffee and watch it play out in front

of me. No one can get out of Fiona's without a conversation with her.

It gives me the chance to give Kirby another once-over. She's about the last person I would've expected to end up here in Aberlach.

The work boots she's wearing look brand-new. Not a scuff on them. Her jeans are formfitting, hugging every one of her curves, as does the plain black T-shirt she's got on.

I'm noticing things about her that I dinnae want to be noticing. I dinnae need to get wrapped up in some woman who probably has no plans to stick around. That will only end in disaster for me.

I've had enough disaster to last me a lifetime.

"Callum."

Kirby is holding a cup of tea and a scone as she takes the seat opposite me. She was with Fiona so long, she didnae have to wait to be served.

Figures.

"I see you've now met Fiona."

Kirby smiles at me before sipping on her tea. "Was told that if I wanted a tour of town, I should ask you."

"Me?" I sputter over my own drink. "Why me?"

"I was told you know everything."

Christ. Fiona cannae keep her nose out of anything. "It's been a minute since I've been here. I dinnae know about knowing everything. Why dinnae we get down to business, aye?"

"Sure, business."

Kirby shifts, her foot grazing my leg. A feeling I'm not used to simmers in my veins at the slight touch. Coughing, I shift to break the contact and get my head where it needs to be.

"Are you sure you want to help me? I don't want you to

feel like you have to," Kirby tells me before I can get a word in. "I'll let you off the hook."

"I dinnae have anything else to do." I shrug a shoulder, leaning back in the chair that is too small for me.

"Like I said, you don't have to help."

"Based on the way I saw ye wielding that sledgehammer? I think I do." I rip a piece of the buttery off and pop it in my mouth. Fuck, that's good. Maybe I should get up earlier just to score one of these every morning.

"But you don't want to."

"Are you always this agreeable?" I ask her.

"Are you always this *disagreeable*?" she throws back at me.

"I said I'd help, lass."

"Against your will." Kirby gives me a syrupy-sweet smile as she eats her own breakfast.

"Show me yer plans." There's no sense in arguing about this. This woman scares me a fuck ton less than me mum. If I dinnae help, she'll eat me alive.

Some things are not worth it.

"Why should I if you don't want to help?" Kirby leans across the table.

Don't roll yer eyes, Callum.

"You know, it disnae hurt to ask for help sometimes." Even if it's advice I dinnae take.

"Maybe if I asked someone who knew what they were doing."

"Ouch." I laugh. "I'm more than a pretty face, lass."

I dinnae miss the way her eyes dip lower, settling on my mouth, before flipping back up to meet my gaze. I want to ask her what she's thinking, but maybe it's better that I dinnae know.

"Okay, fine," she grumbles. "Here's what I want to do."

Pulling out her phone, Kirby unlocks it, taps away, and then passes it over to me. An all modern kitchen fills the screen with white countertops and stainless steel appliances.

While it's stunning, it widnae work in a bed and breakfast like she's planning.

"This winnae work in there, lass."

"And why not?" She quirks a brow at me, looking down at the picture on her phone.

"That all white? You cannae. It'll get ruined immediately."

"How?"

"You plan on serving guests, right?" I finish the last of my coffee and wave one of the servers over for a refill.

"That is the goal of a bed and breakfast, yes," she deadpans.

"You might want something that can withstand more wear and tear. What about…a soapstone?"

Taking out my own phone, I pull up a picture and slide it over to her. "This would look good and withstand the amount of cooking you would need to do."

"Me?" Kirby looks flabbergasted like I just asked her to fly to the moon. "I don't plan on doing the cooking."

"You dinnae?" My cup gets filled, and I nod my thanks as I pull it toward me for another drink.

"Do you think I can cook? I don't have the first clue on what I need to do."

"Then how are you gonna run this bed and breakfast?"

"Well, I was planning on fixing it up to sell it."

"Sell?" I question.

Kirby nods, sipping on her drink. "My life is back in LA. As soon as a few things get cleared up back there, I'll be heading back. So whoever buys this place should know what they're doing."

"Okay. Putting aside who will actually be doing the cooking in the kitchen, I think this would look better."

She takes my phone, her fingertips brushing against mine. Christ, why am I feeling the things I'm feeling with her? Wanting to feel them in more places. My chest. My legs. My cock.

Shite. I need to not be having these thoughts in the middle of Fiona's bakery, but here we are.

"How do you know this will withstand the cooking that will need to be done? Do you have experience running your own restaurant?"

"Do you have a need to prove me wrong?" I ask, leaning across the table into her space. Maybe it's because she's a redhead, but that fiery personality of hers? It's so easy to poke. "I had it at my old place."

"Your old place? I thought you lived here."

"With me mum?"

"I don't know."

"Not everyone is inept in the kitchen. Maybe Mum needs to show you how to cook."

"Why not you?" Kirby leans closer to me. This close, I can see the dark green that rims her eyes. When the light catches them, they are fucking gorgeous. "You don't think you're up for the challenge?"

"Oh, I can show you how to cook."

"Then why did you offer your mom?"

Maybe because being in the same room with her for too long would drive me mad. Or we'd fight the entire time. And I would enjoy that too damn much. But somehow, I cannae resist the chance in spite of my misgivings.

"I'll show you if you think you're ready for it."

"Oh, I'm ready."

"Good." I waggle my brows at her. "So, soapstone then?"

"Soapstone it is. Care to offer any other opinions on my ideas?"

"Gladly, lass. I would love to." I grab my mug and take a sip.

"You don't have to be such a smart-ass about it."

"Wasn't trying to be."

"Sure." Kirby pulls a sleek, silver laptop out of her bag and opens it up. Punching at the keys, she spins it in my direction. "These are the ideas I've had."

Image after image fills the screen of similar manor houses found throughout Scotland. Tartan wallpaper. Wood panel wainscoting. Deep, jewel-color tones painted on the walls. Exposed wood floors. Oversized chairs. Gold, antique accent pieces. It's everything that a B&B should be.

Well, at least from what I can assume. I've never had the pleasure of staying in any…because why would I when I have the money for a modern hotel with amenities?

It makes me sound like an bawbag. Because I was one. At least I have the balls to admit it.

Now?

Now, I'm just trying to figure out my next move.

Focusing my attention back on her computer screen, I tell her, "I think most of these are doable."

Tourists will fucking love this. If they're here visiting the Highlands, she'll be fighting them off with a broom at the door.

"You really think we can do it?" There's a hint of hope in her voice.

"I don't see why not. Some wallpaper, some paint. Should fix things right up."

Fuck, everything in that house just needs a good scrub down and we should have it ready to go in a few weeks. Except that kitchen. That needs some work along with the lounge. They are in the worst condition of all.

A smile lights up Kirby's face. It has her freckles dancing with happiness.

I like the fact that I put it there.

"We might need some more help with the kitchen."

Kirby nods. "I figured I'd hire someone to help with that. There's too much to do in there for just us."

Us. I like that she's already including me in getting the house ready. How quickly she changed her mind.

"Okay then. We've got a plan," Kirby tells me.

"I guess we do," I confirm.

I spin her computer back to her and she makes to grab it from me, her hand lingering over mine.

She makes no move to pull back, so I dinnae either.

"So the lounge and first floor and then we'll be able to work on all the bedrooms."

Christ, just thinking about bedrooms has me thinking of her spread out on a bed. All that red hair of hers against a pillow as I fuck into her.

Damn it. I am not doing a good job of keeping my emotions in check around this woman. Why cannae I keep my thoughts above the belt?

I'm only supposed to be helping her fix up the lodge. That's it. Nothing more. Nothing less.

Now if I can get my dick on board, we'll be square.

Chapter Nine

CALLUM

"Well, I'll be. What's all this?"

Mum walks into the kitchen in her dressing gown and slippers, a look of shock on her face.

"Cannae a man make breakfast?" I grab an old ceramic mug from the open shelf and pour her a cup of coffee.

"They can, but not ye."

I'm already on my second cup as the timer dings. Grabbing the tea towel, I pull the sausage rolls out of the oven. It's one of the few things I've mastered cooking. The spicy flavors of the sausage roll are why I love them so much. These things are a dime a dozen here, but it's something I wanted to learn how to make. It made me feel not completely useless.

"Well, I thought I'd make ye breakfast."

"What have ye done with my son?" The look of shock only grows on her face.

"Christ, Mum. Cannae I make breakfast without it being a big deal?"

Mum shakes her head, reaching across the bunker to

grab a piping hot roll. There's a twinkle in her eye. "Ye're dressed for work. Wanting to impress Kirby?"

"What? Nae."

Mum casts a wary eye over me. It's early. Earlier than I've been up in ages. I even managed to drag a comb through my hair before pulling the long strands back into place in a small bun to keep it out of my eyes while working.

The old sweatshirt I dug out of my closet is torn up. It's not like I'm dressed to meet the King for lunch. I'm dressed to help Kirby with the house.

Nothing more.

"Are you going to take her breakfast? It'd be the neighbourly thing to do."

"I do have manners, Mum."

She scoffs. "Sometimes I wonder."

Grabbing a few rolls, I drop them into a brown paper bag and close the distance between us. "Didnae learn them from you."

"Arse." She swats at me.

"Love ye, Mum."

"You too, my numpty son. Don't forget about practice for the games this afternoon!"

"I winnae."

I laugh as I head out the kitchen door. For once, the weather is perfect. White clouds hang in the sky as the sun makes a rare appearance.

For once, it was easy to wake up. I dinnae dread what I'd be doing today. I don't want to think too much about the reason.

It's been hard to muster much energy for anything lately, but today, I felt the need to make breakfast.

Mainly for me. Not for anyone else.

Especially not the lass standing at the edge of the gate

with Angus staring her down. The look on her face is a cross between amusement and trepidation.

"Mornin'," I call out to her.

"Umm, hi."

Kirby peers at me as I give Angus a pat on the rump.

"I see you've met Angus."

"Angus?"

The cow in question turns back to me, likely smelling what's in my bag. His pale tongue sticks out and he stretches his nose towards me, like he's sniffing the air.

"Ol' man Thomas's Highland cow."

"He looks familiar." Kirby studies him as I ruffle the soft hairs between his oversized horns.

"Met a lot of hairy coos?" I quirk a brow at her.

"Well…"

"Wait, ye have?"

"He looks like the one I met when I kind-of-almost crashed my car."

Angus nudges the bag in my hand, but I ignore him. It's taken a lot of learning to keep from feeding him what he's not supposed to have.

"When did you crash yer car?"

"Almost," Kirby corrects. "It was my first night in town. A tractor nearly ran me over."

I study her as her eyes lock on to mine. "Where did this happen?"

"Before I got to town."

"Aye."

"What?" Kirby plants her hands on her hips, like she's got an attitude about my response. "Why do you say it like that?"

"My guess is you dinnae know how to drive here?" I quirk a brow at her and hand over the bag.

"What are these?" Kirby does her best to ignore me.

If she disnae want to acknowledge that she cannae drive here—likely not knowing what the passing places are—I'll let her have it.

"Sausage rolls."

Kirby fishes one out and takes a hearty bite. "Oh my God. This is amazing. Did you get these from Fiona's?"

"Cheeky shit. I made these."

"You did?" Kirby's eyes widen as she takes another bite, letting out a groan. "Fuck me, they're amazing."

It's a good thing Angus is between us, because it lets me shift the growing problem in my pants.

"Where did Angus come from?" Kirby asks, licking her fingers as she finishes the last bite. "And next question, can I have a second?"

"By all means," I tell her. "He's ol' man Thomas's. His farm is on the edge of town, and there's a hole in the fence. Angus likes people, so he spends his days wandering around. Dinnae you?" I ask the orange-haired cow.

Angus, getting tired of not getting any food, nudges Kirby's hand, and she drops the other half of her sausage roll. The beast snatches it from the ground before wandering back off down the hill.

"That was mine!" she shouts after him.

Laughter barks out of me. "That's Angus for you."

"He's okay just wandering around?" Kirby asks, turning to head back to the inn.

"Aye. Everyone in town knows him. We all look after him."

Once we're back inside, Kirby drops the bag on the small desk that looks to be the check-in desk. The sounds of workers in the kitchen filter their way out here. Since we made the plan last week, we were able to get a crew in here and start right away.

"Even you?"

I close the distance between us. With the bag behind her, my arm brushes against hers as I fish out my own roll. I dinnae miss the way Kirby's teeth sink into her bottom lip.

Christ. This woman is going to be the end of me with the way she's reacting.

A crash in one of the rooms has me jumping away from her.

"Let me go check on that."

Kirby dashes away, clearing the fog that she always seems to bring out in me. Grabbing my roll, I head into the lounge and take stock of everything that needs to be done.

With the half wall now gone, we need to repair the wall it was attached to before refinishing the wood panels. It looks like Kirby has already started cleaning the walls based on the bucket of soapy water sitting on a towel in the middle of the room.

Even a small scrub has helped immensely. As soon as we can get the wall finished, all it will need is a coat of paint and it should be ready to go.

Well, that and fixing up the fireplace hearth.

"Sorry, the guys in the kitchen dropped the old oven."

"Right. So where are we starting in here today?" I ask, brushing off my hands as I finish the last of my own breakfast and glance at the TV in the corner playing a cooking show.

"I'm going to start cleaning if you want to mix the plaster to fix the area where the half wall was connected."

"Aye."

"'Aye?' Just like that? No discussion or argument?" Kirby crosses her arms, staring up at me.

I shrug a shoulder. "It's a good plan."

"Why are you being so agreeable?"

I run a hand through my hair, but it gets stuck in the

bun. Fuck. I forgot I pulled it back already. "Would you like me to be more disagreeable?"

"It's weird. You being nice."

"Fine. Yer plan is terrible."

"That's more like it." Except Kirby's green eyes are sparkling. "Get to work, Callum."

"Right away."

The way she commands me to get to work leaves no room for argument. Knowing I would need to do this, I looked up a few videos on wall repair. It's not the easiest thing I've ever done, but I can at least figure it out while Kirby works on cleaning the walls so we can paint. Based on what she showed me, it's going to be a deep green color.

The noise carries on around me as I work. Until she bumps into me.

"You okay?" I ask, dropping the trowel into the bucket of plaster.

"Look." Kirby drops down next to me.

My gaze follows hers, and the damn rooster has wandered into the house. I don't know how I missed his crowing as he stops in front of the TV.

Staring.

He's transfixed at the show where a baker is making a wedding cake for some famous person. I huvnae paid any attention to it, as it was just on in the background.

"I don't think I've ever heard Mr. Peep so quiet," Kirby whispers.

"Is this why you call him that?"

"Yes. What do you call him?"

"Mainly an annoying fucker." Kirby swats at my stomach. "Did you discover the secret to getting him to shut up?"

"I think we did."

"Better than cooking him."

"Callum!" she hisses. "You are not allowed to kill my rooster."

"I had no such intentions." I laugh.

We're both squatting, watching this crazy rooster stare at the TV. My large frame almost overtakes her. I seriously dinnae know what it is about this woman, but every time I'm around her, I just want to pull her into my arms and keep her there.

I huvnae felt this way in a long time. It's disturbing that of all people, it's this interloper that's come crashing into my life who makes me feel things.

I dinnae think I felt this way about my wife towards the end. Probably why she ran off with all of my money.

"Let's get out of here so we don't disturb him."

Kirby stands too quickly and ends up crashing into me, sending us both tumbling to the floor.

Where she lands smack-dab on top of me.

Fuck.

All that crazy mess of hair falls around our faces, blocking out every single thing except for her face.

The face that I huvnae been able to stop thinking about since she got to Aberlach. Her eyes widen, and I dinnae miss the way her tongue darts out to lick her bottom lip.

Shit, is she feeling the same things that I am? It widnae take much for me to lean up and close the distance between us.

Fuck, should I kiss her? Would that be weird?

God, why am I being so…wishy-washy about this?

If you want to kiss her, Callum, kiss her.

Instead, I reach up and tuck her hair behind her ear, resting my hand on her face. My thumb brushes against the apple of her cheek. I dinnae miss the way she shudders as I keep my hand there.

Her skin is so damn soft. I wonder what she would taste like. Would she taste as good as she smells?

Fuck. Now the only thing I can think about is how this woman tastes. I dinnae know if I'm going to be able to get that thought out of my head.

Except a crashing noise completely pulls me out of the moment as Kirby spins off me.

"Callum. Kirby?"

Of course. Of *fucking* course. Mum's voice rings out through the house, sending Mr. Peep squawking, fleeing the same way he came in.

Mum would be a cockblock over the actual cock, Mr. Peep.

Kirby is furiously trying to right herself, the blush on her face evidence of the things she seems to be feeling.

I dinnae know, but either way, I'm pissed as hell that Mum chose this moment to walk in here.

"Henry called. Ye're late for practice."

"Oh fuck."

"What practice?" Kirby asks, hopping up to her feet like nothing happened. "Practice for what?"

"For the Highland Games." A conversation I dinnae really want to be having with her right now.

"The Highland what now?" A gleeful smile crosses her face.

"Oh, Kirby. You'll have to join us. They are the most fun, hen," Mum tells her.

Christ. Of course she invites her to this.

"Mum. Kirby disnae need to come."

"I see you're agreeable with everyone." She smirks. Her green eyes are twinkling. God, she really is fucking gorgeous.

Mum waves me off, heading to Kirby and wrapping an arm around her shoulders. "I'll make sure to bring you with me. The whole town comes out. Bagpipers. Field games. Food and drinks. It's a right good time. Why dinnae we let Callum get to practice and then I'll tell you more about the Highland Games over a nice cup of tea?"

Mum links an arm through hers and pulls her out of the lounge. I cannae help but stare at Kirby as she leaves, then turns back to me, a smile firmly etched in place.

Fuck, I really need to get whatever I'm feeling towards her under control because this cannae happen.

No way.

Not a chance in hell am I going to develop feelings for this woman who came breezing into my life.

Too late for that, you bawbag.

Chapter Ten

KIRBY

"Kirby. How are ye?" Thomas greets me as I open the door to the hardware store. "How are things going up at the house?"

"Good," I tell him, even though it is definitely a much bigger project than I originally had planned for. "Callum's been a big help."

More agreeable than I anticipated. Especially when I thought he was going to kiss me the other day. If only Miriam hadn't walked in.

Would I have let him kiss me?

There's not a chance in hell I would've pushed him away. I've been imagining what his lips would feel like. Are they as soft as they look? Would his beard leave behind marks as he devoured me?

It's all I've been thinking about. It left me tossing and turning all night. And with no vibrator in sight, I had to take matters into my own hands.

With thoughts of Callum leading the way.

"Glad to hear he's so helpful," Thomas tells me,

bringing me out of my wayward thoughts. "Easing into life in Aberlach?"

He's following me around the store as I get more of the supplies I need to tackle the day's projects.

I give him a warm smile. "Still adjusting. What I wouldn't give for a good taco."

He barks out a laugh at that. "Gotta head up to the city for that."

"Maybe I'll try that this weekend, then," I tell him.

Even though it's a big fat lie. I've been walking everywhere I can because to be honest? The roads here terrify me. Attempting them for a second time, I was convinced another car was going to collide with me head-on. Maybe if I took the time to learn these damn one-lane roads, it might be better.

But all my time is spent at the lodge, trying to make it presentable to sell.

That and ignoring my burly neighbor. Even if it's hard as hell with him in my space.

Because now? Now all I want to do is kiss him. Maybe roll around in the sheets with him.

But I don't tell him that.

"If it isn't my newest favorite townsperson."

Spinning on my heel, I find Miriam striding into the store with a purpose. One that looks like it's the man standing beside me.

"Thomas. Have the batteries come in yet for the smoke alarm?"

"Aye. Let me help ye, Miriam." Thomas turns to me. "Take what ye need and I'll add it to your tab, Kirby."

"Thanks, Thomas. Nice to see you, Miriam."

"Ye stop by for lunch now, okay?" she tells me. "Ye're withering away."

I smile at her, because this is not the first time I've

heard this. Who knew demo on a house could work up such a sweat? Not one of the more pleasurable ways I've done it, but it feels good to be fixing up a space like this.

Trudging back up the hill toward the manor house, it looks different in the bright sunshine. Almost like I have what it takes to make this work. Like it's telling me I can do it.

My lungs are burning from the steep walk as I head in the side door to the lounge. Even taking down the one wall has opened the room up.

I've never been one for a lot of home décor—opting for a more modern, minimalist approach for my apartment. But here, I want to add more.

More details. More paint. Cushy furniture that makes people feel welcome. At least, that's the plan for when I sell it. The homier it feels, the more inviting it will be for any potential buyers.

Dropping my supplies in the middle of the room, I get to work. Small samples of paint are splashed across the upper half of the walls. Do I want a combination? Or just one color?

With the bright sunshine coming in near the bay window, the darker colors will really shine through.

Grabbing another one of the paint samples I picked up today, I grab a large amount on my brush before slapping it on the wall. The slightest pressure from the paint brush pushes a hole through the plaster. It disintegrates on contact. And what's worse? A bird comes flying through the hole.

"Ahh! Fuck me!" I shout. It's flapping around the lounge before it takes a nosedive toward me. "What the hell?"

Ducking, I cover my head with my arms and pray that it makes it out one of the open windows.

Can one thing go right with this house?

The toilet exploded on me. Who knows the condition of the rest of the walls, and now a bird is flapping around in the lounge. Am I going to need to tear down every wall just to make sure that no animals are nesting inside?

Maybe I can't do this. Maybe this is my sign from the universe that I need to pack up and head home with my tail between my legs.

Except there's nothing for me to go home to. If I went back now, all I would do is stay at my mom's and wonder what the hell is going on at work and *if* I'll be arrested for something I didn't do.

Anger over everything going on right now is rising to the surface. Grabbing the sledgehammer, I head into one of the front bedrooms. I know where a wall needs to come down, and this is the perfect time to deal with it.

This terrible floral wallpaper? Gone. The hideous sconces? Out. The wall that blocks the door from fully opening?

The perfect excuse for my rage.

The burn in my muscles as the head connects with the wall is welcome. At least this one doesn't have any animals coming out of it.

Although, I shouldn't even think it. I don't want to tempt fate.

Each slam against the wall has more and more of my anger wilting away. Until that voice. That voice that gets me worked up into a tizzy.

"Everything okay in here?"

I don't turn back as Callum comes into the room.

"What do you think?" I fire another crack into the wall.

"If I tell the truth, are you going to turn that thing on me?"

"Tempting, but no."

Another crack. More plaster coming down.

"What's wrong, Kirby?"

The way Callum says my name shouldn't be as enticing as it is. Like he really is asking and wants to know why I'm in the mood I'm in. The lilt of his accent does funny things to my insides.

But I push all of that aside as I throw another swing into the wall.

"What isn't wrong? I'm accused of stealing money from my job and put on leave. I inherited a house in a country that I can't seem to make heads or tails of. I haven't had a good night's sleep since I got here because damn Mr. Peep won't stop waking me up." It all comes out in a verbal diarrhea. It feels good to let it all out along with each pound of the hammer.

"Is that all?"

I give the wall one last solid throw. Damn, does that feel good. "No! Why can't I find a good fucking taco in this country?!" I shout, dropping the hammer.

I've been here for two weeks. It's too early to admit defeat. Would it be easier to call up my lawyer and have him sell this place? Sure.

But that's not in my nature. I don't give up. I don't *want* to give up.

"Are you done?" Callum asks.

"Yes." I breathe out, sucking more air into my lungs.

"Good. Then I'm going to kiss you now."

Callum closes the distance between us and takes my face in his rough, calloused hands. I wasn't sure I'd love the feel of them on my skin, but I do.

Anticipation ripples between us as I hold on to his wrists, my eyes locked on his.

"Can I?" he whispers.

Licking my lips, I nod.

Because right now, there is nothing I want more than to feel Callum's lips on mine.

The kiss is soft, hesitant. Nothing like I imagined kissing this man to be.

And believe you me, I've imagined it.

"Is that all you got?" I whisper when he pulls back.

Those playful blue eyes of his are sparkling. His thumb brushes my lower lip. Desire swirls in the room around us. My hands drift down his strong forearms to fist in his tight T-shirt.

I only see the smirk playing on his lips before his mouth crashes down on mine.

This. *This* is the kiss I've imagined. The way his hand fists in my hair. The slight bite of pain as he ravages my mouth.

It's a give and take. Learning what we like and don't like. Callum swallows every one of my whimpers. Every moan.

I feel each stroke of his tongue against mine low in my belly. An ache that I've never felt before in my life has me wanting to climb this man like a tree.

I'm desperate for more as Callum slows the kiss, drifting his lips down my jaw. His beard tickles my neck. God, what I wouldn't give to feel that between my legs. To have him lick my pussy as he makes me come harder than I've ever come in my life.

I'm assuming. Because based on the strength of this man, there's no way he wouldn't make me black out from pleasure.

"God," I whine. "Oh my God."

Callum's hand drifts down my side and settles on my ass, pulling me in closer to him. Him and his very hard cock.

"Want to know something, lass?" he whispers against my neck as he sucks on my throbbing pulse there.

"What?" It comes out breathless. Callum has sucked all common sense from me. He's drawn every bit of air from the room. I'm not breathing clear air in. Only Callum.

"I've felt like this since the very first moment I met you."

Callum lifts me onto the dresser in the room and steps between my open legs. It gives me the opportunity to take in his disheveled appearance. All that hair of his is a mess. Blue eyes wide with need. Sneaking a glance at the growing problem in his pants, I can't deny that he's big. I want to feel him inside of me.

Cupping his cheek, I bring his attention back to me and kiss him again. This time, it's not as hurried, but no less intense.

My free hand drifts down his shirt and skirts under the soft material. The hard abs I find there ripple under my touch. Callum pulls me closer to him, grinding at the apex of my thighs.

I seriously don't know if I would survive sex with this man. Callum might destroy me.

What a way to go.

Callum tips me back, and that's when a very loud, very distinct crow echoes through the house.

"Fuck me," Callum whispers, burying his face in my neck. "That damn rooster."

"Is it too late to cook him?" I mutter, not meaning it.

"Harsh." Callum presses one last kiss to my neck before he pulls back, adjusting his pants. I fight the groan that threatens to escape at not feeling that inside me. "And I thought I was the only one that wanted to cook him."

Seeing Callum like this makes me want to say fuck it to

my plans of destroying this room and instead take him up to my room.

Fucking Mr. Peep. He comes strutting into the room like he owns the place. I guess he's had the run of it since no one has been here the last few years. But could he have picked a worse time to make an appearance?

"Fitting of the crime."

"Why don't we lay off the rooster homicide today and get back to the work we actually need to do?"

"Fine," I grumble. "Way to be the voice of reason."

Callum helps me off the dresser, but his hand lingers on my waist. Being this close to him is messing with my head.

God forbid, am I actually starting to like him? Do I know him well enough to like him? Or do I just want to screw him to get these feelings out of my system?

The smile lingering on his too handsome face has me stirring.

"What?"

His fingers trail down my neck, causing goose bumps to break out all over my skin. "You said something about a taco?"

Laughter burbles up inside of me. Why should I need a taco when Callum MacRae is kissing me like I'm the best thing in the world? "What taco?"

Chapter Eleven

CALLUM

"Do you think this paint color will work in here?" Kirby asks.

With the samples taped to the wall in the dining room, Kirby waves me in so I can give my opinion.

I wipe the sweat from my brow. Renovating a house is not an easy task. Especially when I've spent many a sleepless night dreaming about Kirby. Even more so now that I know what it's like to kiss her.

"I think it looks good."

Kirby rolls those beautiful green eyes at me. "Is that your honest opinion? Or are you just saying that so you can kiss me again?"

Smiling at her, I stalk towards her, closing the small space between us. "Lass, do ye really think I'd lie to you?"

I take her into my arms, watching as the smile spreads across her face. "Do you think I'm being agreeable to be agreeable?" I ask.

"I wouldn't put it past you."

"Never." I shake my head. "You wouldn't like it if I did that."

"See, now you're being agreeable." Kirby smiles up at me.

"Maybe I want to be agreeable just to see you smile."

That earns me an eye roll. "What a cheese ball."

"Well, you are the one with the strong opinions here."

Kirby's hands dip lower into the waistband of my pants. "And I would like yours, Callum."

"I think it's too dark."

"What?" This has Kirby pulling out of my arms. "It is not!"

The shriek in her voice is high.

"You asked. I'm only telling you my opinion."

"So much for being agreeable," Kirby mutters.

"Look." I shift Kirby to look at the back of the dining room that leads into the kitchen. "There's not much natural light in here. You want to do a few shades lighter to brighten the room up."

Kirby steps out of my arms and heads to the part of the kitchen where I told her it was too dark. She's studying the space. Since it's the weekend, the guys she found to help with the kitchen aren't working.

It's just the two of us in here.

"Do you think it blends in with the lounge?"

She steps out of the dining room, where there's a small bar that leads into the open room. One that's coming along thanks to our hard work.

"Does it need to blend?"

The lounge is going to be decorated in deep greens. With the wood paneling, it'll be fucking gorgeous once it all comes together.

"Okay, I thought you were trying to be agreeable," Kirby complains.

"Enough with this agreeable shit," I tell her. "You want

my opinion, and I think it's fine. Do something lighter in the kitchen and it'll be fine in here. Aye?"

"And it'll go with the vibe I'm going for?"

"Old time Scotland? Aye."

"God, are you trying to be even sexier?"

Kirby's hands rest on her hips. The way she's standing there, the sunbeams from the lounge casting her in a low glow, she looks angelic.

Fucking beautiful.

"I dinnae think I have to try." I smirk at her. There's a good amount of space between us, neither one of us making a move to close it.

"You and that accent?" Kirby waves a hand around, as if to signal she's annoyed with me. "You don't even have to try."

"What can I say? It comes naturally."

Kirby looks like she wants to murder me. It's no surprise. We've been butting heads since she got here.

I don't know why fighting with her is such foreplay.

There is an open can of paint sitting next to her, and by the looks of it, she's eyeing it to decide if she can lob it at me.

"I dare you."

"You what?" A menacing look crosses her face. "You think I won't do it?"

Kirby takes a step closer to it.

"Oh, I know you will." Instead of moving closer to the paint, Kirby steps closer to me. "I dinnae doubt ye for a second, lass."

Tension hangs heavy in the air. One strike of a match and the heat between the two of us could explode.

Kirby walks by it, dragging her finger along the rim of it. She's thinking about it. I know she is.

"I have a better idea."

"You do?"

She nods. "I do. I think you might like it."

"Aye?"

She taps a finger against her pillow-soft lips. Lips I've wanted to get my own again and again. It sends my thoughts south, imagining that sexy-as-sin mouth of hers wrapping around my cockhead and taking me in long, slow sucks.

"Why don't you come over here and find out what I have in mind for us?"

What little resistance I have snaps like a twig.

I'm not sure which of us moves first, but our mouths search the other's out as we consume one another.

Finally.

Fucking *finally*.

Chapter Twelve

KIRBY

Oh God. This is happening. *Again.*

The feel of Callum's lips on my neck is enough to send me into the stratosphere. Callum is overwhelming in every way.

Egging him on was the easiest thing to do. He could have done it to me and I would have snapped.

A person can only have so much willpower against a man like Callum. Because I am ready for this man to absolutely devour me.

His lips trail a warm path of kisses across my collarbone, and everything about the moment is perfect. The smell of his shampoo. The way his fingertips are digging into my hips. The friction of his beard as it scratches against me.

"Callum."

"Fucking delicious, Kirby."

"I want you." Wrapping a leg around his thighs, I pull him in closer. And the feel of his dick pressing into my stomach? I can't wait until it's inside me. Filling me. Stretching me.

I let out a greedy moan, wanting all of it.

"Upstairs," I breathe out.

"No," Callum bites out. "I need to have you right here."

Setting me on the sofa in the lounge, he drops to his knees. Those blue eyes of his are lit up with hunger. His teeth are digging into his bottom lip as he studies me, like he's trying to figure out how to make me come first time.

The thought of Callum giving me multiple orgasms has me on edge and ready to explode.

"Hands on the back of the couch," Callum demands while pulling my ass to the edge of the sofa. I reach back behind me and hold on.

Those big strong hands of his grasp the waistband of my yoga pants and slide them down and off my legs. Callum licks his way up one leg, bypassing my aching pussy, then giving the same attention to the other leg.

"Do you know how sexy you are, bonny lass?" Callum nibbles on the tender skin of my thigh.

"Not as sexy as you."

I fight every urge to sink my fingers into his long hair. To bring his mouth to where I really want it. But the teasing nips and bites are amping up my pleasure.

"Callum, please," I beg. "Please."

He leans back on his heels, and a satisfied smirk sits on his mouth. "Do you know what that does to me? Hearing you beg?"

"Will it get your mouth on me?"

Callum kisses my inner thigh, not quite where I want him. "Like that?"

"Higher."

"Here?" he asks, pressing a kiss into the soft material of my shirt.

"Callum!" I whine.

Deft fingers start to unbutton my shirt. His fingers brushing over the skin he's exposing, inch by inch, have goose bumps breaking out all over me.

"Fuck. These breasts? Perfect."

I drop my head back as he showers me with praise. His hands are roaming, pushing the shirt down my shoulders. The slight sting of his beard as he buries his face in my cleavage has me arching off the couch. When his mouth closes over one satin-covered nipple, I nearly explode.

"Keep doing that."

"Aye." Callum pulls the cup of my bra down, blowing warm air over my hardened tip. He shifts his attention between both of my breasts, and it makes me crazy.

I want to feel his mouth everywhere. To have him mark every inch of my skin. Claim me as his.

When he moves his focus farther south, I'm so strung out, I'm ready to come.

Callum drags his nose up the soft cotton of my underwear. "How wet are you for me, lass?"

"Why don't you take them off and find out?"

A sly smile spreads across his face before he sits back on his heels again. Hooking a finger, he drags it up and down, brushing against my clit before ripping them off me.

Callum attacks my pussy with a fervor I've never felt. The way his tongue slides inside me ignites a white-hot lust. It's blinding in its potency as his fingers strum over my clit.

Fingers digging into the back of the couch, I do everything not to reach out to him. To guide him. But he doesn't need my help. Callum knows exactly what he's doing to get me there.

"I'm so close."

"That's it. C'mon, lass. I want you to come on my tongue. I want to drink up every drop of your release."

The vibrations against me have me exploding. Stars dance behind my eyes as my body feels like it's on fire at Callum's touch. Strong hands hold me to him as he does exactly what he said—drinking up every ounce of my orgasm.

"Holy fuck. That was…that was…"

Callum sits back, wiping his mouth with the back of his hand. "Amazing?"

"More than that. Fucking incredible."

I'm boneless as Callum stands and reaches behind him to pull off his shirt. He undoes his pants and shoves them down his strong legs. It frees his long, thick cock. It springs out, hitting him in his perfect abs.

"Holy shit." My mouth waters at the sight of Callum standing naked in front of me.

"Like it?" He gives himself a gentle stroke.

"You know I do."

Callum steps closer. "What are you going to do about it?"

Sitting up, I knock his hand away and wrap my much smaller hand around his girth. His eyes hood over as I lean closer and lick the precum away from the tip.

"Mmm."

I trace a finger down the long vein on the underside of his cock. It's big. The bulbous head of his uncut cock is purple, likely aching to get inside my mouth.

"Are ye just going to stare at it?"

Waggling my eyebrows at him, I take as much of him into my mouth as I can. The way I stretch my mouth around him makes my pussy ache for him.

My hand and mouth work together to get Callum off. He thickens in my mouth, and it has me rubbing my legs together to keep myself from coming again. Because the next time that happens is going to be with Callum inside me.

"Alright, lass." Callum wraps his hand in my hair and pulls me off him. "Christ, you look fucking sexy. Mouth all red from taking me."

"Are you going to fuck me?" I ask as he swipes his thumb over my swollen lips.

"Aye."

Callum hauls me into his arms before spinning me to press my back to his front. I hear the telltale signs of a condom wrapper as he suits up.

"Are you ready?" he asks, sliding that hard length between my legs.

"Yes. God, yes."

Callum bends me in half over the couch before lining himself up and thrusting inside.

"Oooh."

Callum doesn't move as he lets me adjust to his size. It's been awhile since I've been with a guy. Work always came first.

But if there was someone like Callum at home? I would've made more of a point to do this.

"Ready?"

"Yes." I wiggle my hips ever so slightly to let him know that I'm good.

"You feel amazing." Callum pulls out before slamming back inside. Every time he thrusts back in, my need for the man ratchets up even higher.

Callum's moans hit my ears, letting me know he wants this just as much as I do.

He pulls me up so that my back is flush to his chest. Not a breath of air can get between us as his hand drifts up past my breasts to close around my neck.

"Do you know how good you feel? Fuck, Kirby," he growls into my ear. "So. Fucking. Good."

Callum's accent is heavy with lust.

"Gah!" I'm so blissed out that when I finally tip over the edge, I'm thankful I'm in Callum's arms, otherwise I would collapse. "Fuck, Callum!"

"Yessss. That's it, lass."

Callum's fingers dig in even harder as he continues pumping inside me until he comes on a roar. "Fuck!"

The room smells of sex and sweat as the two of us come down from our highs. Callum pulls out, taking care of the condom before settling us both on the sofa. His arms wrap around me, dragging soft fingers up and down my overheated skin.

"That was fucking amazing, Kirb."

I nuzzle into his side, nipping at the underside of his jaw. "I hope you know that I want you to do that again."

"As many times as you wish."

Chapter Thirteen

CALLUM

There's a pleasant ache in my body as someone in bed stirs next to me. The kind of ache and soreness that comes after spending the night wrapped around someone.

That someone being Kirby. Her long eyelashes kiss the tops of her cheeks. That mouth of hers—always so set on proving me wrong—is open, breathing deeply.

Stunning. It's the only way I can describe her like this. After spending all day together, we tried to make progress on the house, but didnae. With more paint ending up on the floor than the walls, we decided it was time to clean up.

Together.

Which ended with the two of us in bed together.

Mist hangs low on the lawn, obscuring the view of the loch beyond. I have no idea what time it is, but Mr. Peep makes his presence known.

"Fuck me," I groan, rolling over into the warmth that is Kirby.

"I'm going to kill him," Kirby mutters, burrowing even farther into my chest.

"No killing Mr. Peep." I drop a kiss on the top of her head. Even if I want to do it myself. "Cooking shows, remember?"

"Ugh. I just want to stay in bed with you."

Flipping Kirby onto her back, I nestle myself between her legs. Pillow lines mar her face. "While I'd love that, we have to work on the house. And the games are coming up this weekend."

"And I get to go, right?"

"Aye." I nip at her lip. "I don't think I could keep you away."

Kirby smiles, a sleepy, happy smile. "You couldn't. I want to see you in a kilt."

"You already have."

"I didn't see anything good."

"Cheeky lass." I tickle her sides, turning her into a squirming mess.

"Stop it!" she shrieks, her laughter echoing around the small room. Kirby tries to wiggle out of my hold, but I dinnae let her get far. "You can't blame me for wanting to see the goods."

"Didnae you get your fill yesterday?"

"I don't know if I'll ever have my fill."

That has me taking a kiss from her. Slow and easy. Morning breath be damned. "I'll make sure you get yer own show."

"Good." Kirby stretches under me, the sheet dropping off her breasts, exposing her tight nipples.

All I want is to stay wrapped up with this woman. But I cannae.

"Are you trying to drive me mad?" I ask. Rolling out of bed, I find my boxers and step into them. Kirby makes no bones about her perusal of me. The slow rake of her eyes over me does nothing to cool my morning wood.

"I don't think I have to try very hard."

Dropping my hands on either side of her head, I suck one nipple into my mouth. "Well then, maybe I should do the same to you."

"Callum," Kirby whines.

"Later, lass. You and I have a long day ahead of us."

With it being a new week, the kitchen crew will be back anytime, and I know she wants to try and finish off the lounge sooner rather than later.

Staying in bed all day winnae accomplish that. As much as I want it to happen.

"Will it end with us back here?"

I wink at her. "Aye."

Kirby tosses the sheet to the side and steps out of bed in all her naked glory. She's teasing me, I know it.

Cheeky lass.

I watch as she disappears into the bathroom before coming back and getting dressed. Someone that sexy shouldn't have to wear that many clothes.

Crossing the room, I wrap an arm around her waist and pull her into me.

"You and I are going to work on this house. Do everything we need to today and then after, we'll have dinner and then I'm going to bring you back up here and toss you onto that mattress and fuck yer brains out."

"Is that so?" The need in Kirby's eyes belies the playfulness in her tone.

Oh yeah, she likes that plan.

"Aye. Now, get this pretty arse of yours downstairs so we can get this day started."

Kirby steals a quick kiss from me. It's too short for my liking, but when she fishes out jeans and her ratty T-shirt to get to work, I cannae fault her.

"Good. Get moving, Callum. The sooner we get this day started, the sooner we get back here."

I don't think I've ever moved so fast.

Chapter Fourteen

KIRBY

"Why do you have to leave so early?" I whine, cuddling farther into Callum's side. I've gotten used to my mornings with him. And days.

Well, nights too. I've just gotten used to him.

To Callum.

I never thought that he would blend so seamlessly into my life, but he has. It's like he's always been a part of it.

It hasn't even been that long that I've been here, but I like it. Like the easy pace of life in Aberlach. Getting advice from Thomas on how to fix this place up. Fiona and her pastries.

Callum and, well, everything about him.

Hell, even Mr. Peep.

"We need to practice one more time." His voice is rough as his calloused hand rakes over my bare back.

"Can't they do it without you?" I throw my leg over his hips, feeling his morning length there. I run my hand down his chest, loving the scratchiness from the happy trail that leads to his thick erection. "Don't they know I need you?"

"Christ," he grumbles as I give him one long, slow stroke. "I cannae take you anywhere."

Resting my chin on his chest, I stare up into his blue eyes. His face is still heavy with sleep, but damn, does he ever look sexy.

Especially with the way his hand is drifting down to my bare ass.

"You're not taking me anywhere if you leave me hanging like this."

Callum grabs his phone from the nightstand and checks the time. It's still dark out. "Fuck. I can be a few minutes late."

"Good." I give him a smile, telling him I won as I slide down his body.

I swallow his hard cock down as far as I can. It's taken some work to get here, with how big he is, but I don't mind. I love that I can taste how much he wants me.

My hand and fist work in tandem to take as much of him as possible. His eyes locked on mine, his hand tangled in my hair, and each groan of his all spur me on.

Callum tightens his hold in my hair and pulls me off of him.

"Flip," he commands.

"What?" I look up at him, wiping off my mouth.

"You think I'm the only one that gets to come? Fuck that."

Callum leans over, grabbing my hips and swinging them toward his mouth and, "oooh."

When his lips land on my clit, it takes everything in me not to come right then and there. The precision with which this man uses his tongue should be a crime. Each stroke sends me higher and higher. I'm ready to come.

Until Callum is no longer working me over.

"Why'd you stop?" I moan, turning to look back at him.

"Because you need to start again." He gives a little thrust of his hips, the head of his cock jutting into my chin.

Turning back to look at him, I give him a wicked smile before diving back onto him.

"That's it. God, do you know how fucking good you look on me like this?" Callum's strong hands squeeze the globes of my ass as he devours my pussy.

It's hard to get a good angle on him like this, but wow. I can't remember the last time I've sixty-nined. Not that my past sexual experiences were all that great. They were fine.

Callum? God, I would be just fine doing this and only this with him for the rest of my life, and I would be living on cloud orgasm for eternity.

Shifting slightly so I can take more of him into my mouth, I squeeze his cock harder as he thrusts through my tight fist.

He's getting close. I'm getting close. I want to swallow down his release as he licks up every drop of mine.

I dig my nails into his thigh, letting him know just that. Callum gives my ass a slap, acknowledging that he knows what it means.

It pulls a deep, vibrating moan from my chest. If it's possible, I can feel his smile against my pussy.

Oh yeah. We'll definitely be revisiting that. Feeling his handprint on my ass, marking me, claiming me as his?

I want it.

When Callum's tongue swirls around my clit another time, I can't help it. I explode. Choking around his cock, I do my best to suck in air as I fly off into the stars.

I'm holding on to him for dear life as a few more pulls and licks of the salty head of his dick have him spilling into my mouth. It feels endless. Time has slowed down as I suck up every last drop of his release.

Holy shit. Pulling off him, I rest my head on his thigh as I refill my lungs with air.

Who needs air when you can have an orgasm with Callum?

"Fuck." Callum presses a kiss to the inside of my thigh. "Kirby."

I smile as my eyes close. I love the way he says my name. The lilt of it coming off his tongue.

"Good?"

Callum shifts out from under me and goes into the bathroom to turn on the shower so it can heat up, then comes back and stands beside the bed.

"Fucking amazing."

I sit up and stare at him. In the now early morning light, all his hard edges are soft. Hair hanging around his shoulders. Beard wet. Eyes happy.

Leaning forward, I give his hip my own kiss. Because I don't know if I'll ever have enough of this man.

"Time to clean up."

Heading into the en suite bathroom, I'm a happy, sated mess, and my hair is a wild mess of curls to match. My mouth is red and my eyes still shrouded with lust.

"I dinnae think you've ever looked sexier, lass." Callum comes up behind me and pulls my naked body against his.

Staring into his eyes has a whole swirl of emotions getting stirred up in me. This man has seen me at my literal worst. I mean, what is below being covered in toilet water and mud after getting the boot from your job for embezzling?

Well, suspected embezzling. That's still under investigation, the last I checked in with Joanne.

I should probably check in again, but it's hard to care when I'm so happy here. It doesn't seem to matter right now. Life currently seems so far away from what it was only a few weeks ago.

Maybe this is life's way of telling me to slow down. That maybe that promotion doesn't matter.

Right now, the only thing that matters is the tender way that Callum guides me into the shower. The gentleness of his touch as he cleans me. The softness of his lips as he steals a slow and languid kiss.

I can't get enough of him.

As the shower starts to cool, we get out and I wrap myself in a towel before drying off and sliding into his oversized flannel shirt.

"I'll go start some coffee before you leave."

"Thanks, lass."

I pause while Callum gets dressed and watch as all of his muscles get tucked into the neat uniform of his. I have to shake myself out of my stupor and go do what I said I would.

Callum is getting to me more than I ever thought possible. Instead of spending the day fixing up the house, I'll be picnicking with his mom and her friends at the Highland Games.

The old Kirby could never have imagined taking a day off for something like this. Something so *frivolous*.

The new Kirby? She's giving her old self the middle finger. Because there is nothing I want to do more than spend my day with the people of Aberlach.

The games have been something I wanted to attend since I first heard Miriam mention them. And getting to see Callum in a kilt again? I wouldn't miss it for the world.

The smell of the bitter coffee does wonders to help wake me up as I pull my wet hair back into a braid. I'll deal with that later.

Once it's done brewing, I pour two cups as Callum

comes into the kitchen. Damn… With his hair pulled back and his beard freshly groomed?

Callum MacRae in a kilt is a sight to behold.

"Look at you." I hand him a mug and his fingers close over mine, not moving. It has heat buzzing through my veins that has nothing to do with the hot ceramic under them.

"Like what you see?" His lips curl up into a salacious smile.

"You know I do."

Callum gives me a teasing peck and takes the mug from me, drinking down a hearty pull. "Mmm, perfect."

The heated gaze he gives me has me wishing we could go right back upstairs. But I know better. And hell if Mr. Peep doesn't know it too with his crow that breaks the moment.

"I guess that means I need to move my arse." Callum finishes his coffee and sets the mug in the sink.

"I'll see you there." I sip on my coffee as I watch Callum leave. The way he steps into his finely polished shoes in that kilt is enough to drive any woman wild.

Before he's out the door, he turns and comes back to me, pulling me in close.

"Just try not to go lookin' up any more kilts, aye?"

I laugh. "You're such a bawbag."

"Listen to you."

"You like that? Me insulting you?" I might have picked up a thing or two being here.

Callum drops his forehead to mine, his blue eyes piercing me with his gaze. "Just you. I like you."

I press a quick kiss to his lips. "I like you too. The only kilt I'll be looking up today is yours."

"As it should be."

And then he's out the door. Taking all of my common sense with him.

Because when I landed here, all I wanted was to fix up this house and move on. Use it as a reprieve from my real life since that's in shambles.

Now I have no idea what I want to do.

Damn the man in the kilt that just walked out. Because that's the only thing I can focus on.

Callum.

Right now, it's not the worst thing in the world.

Chapter Fifteen

CALLUM

"Why the fuck are ye so happy?" Henry asks.

The sound of bagpipes can be heard from every spot in town. This likely would have been something I bitched and moaned about in the past.

If I could help it, I never came home for these things. I turned my nose up at this and everything the town did.

If I wasn't making money, then why the fuck would I do it?

It was not the healthiest of mindsets.

Now, being here in the fresh Scottish air on this fall day? There's nowhere I'd rather be. Especially knowing that Kirby will be here later.

"Piss off," I tell him without much force behind it.

"Someone's all loved up." He makes kissing noises which I ignore.

No sense in telling him that a certain redhead has caught my eye.

"Again, piss off, Henry."

"Damn. You really are interested in someone. I don't think I've seen ye like this since uni."

The downside of a small town. Everyone knows everyone. Henry knows all about what brought me back to town. There's no way I could lie to him. He's one of my oldest friends. One of the few that stuck around even when I was a bawbag when I moved to Edinburgh.

"Alright, get into place. We're startin' here," the thick, loud voice of the band leader shouts across our small spot of land where we're waiting to leave.

"Thank fuck," I mutter to myself.

"Dinnae think yer getting out of this." Henry hoists up his instrument and gets into place. "Ye owe me a pint."

"You mean you owe me one," I throw back. "Because last time, you got so pished, I had to haul yer arse home."

He rolls his eyes at me as the first few notes of the song we're playing ring out.

Playing the bagpipes comes easy to me. It's something me granda taught me when I was a wee'un. It was the one thing I could carry on when he died, even if I was a shite player back then. I've improved a lot since then, so it's nice in a way to be back out here today.

As we parade through town, camera phones are pointed in our direction. Everyone is enraptured as brigade after brigade march through the narrow roads towards the fields behind the distillery.

"Ow ow!" The familiar voice breaks through the drone of the bagpipes. Casting my eyes over toward a group of people, I find my mum and Kirby standing with a few of the other women that they'll be lunching with.

I shoot a wink at her as I continue playing my pipes with ease. It gives me an extra burst of confidence as we parade into the main fields. I shouldn't want to impress Kirby as much as I do. She's told me she's only in town to fix up the inn before selling it. The last thing I need is someone breezing in and out of my life.

I know this. I know I shouldn't want a woman who winnae be here when the paint dries. I've had enough women like that to last me a lifetime.

I dinnae think my ex ever would have come home with me for this event. She was all about appearances and money, and maybe that contributed to my mindset these last few years. Always working for her, because otherwise, what kind of husband was I if not providing for her?

Half of the town is already spread out to watch the competitions that are going on in the main fields.

Various stalls line the walkways for people to get trinkets of any kind, and the smells of food are heavenly.

Having not had anything to eat this morning, I'm starving. But, you'll never hear me complain about waking up to mutual orgasms instead of breakfast.

By the time our band finishes, I'm packing up my instrument and watching everyone else walk on by. My ears will be ringing for days with the sound of bagpipes. Our group is only a part of the welcome parade, so my work is done.

I can sit back and enjoy all the hard work that I've put into the games. These last few months huvnae been all that bad. Seeing everything come together is a rewarding feeling. To see so many people, townsfolk and tourists alike, enjoying themselves is a place of pride for me.

Even if I groaned when Mum would get me out of bed to help Fiona. I didnae appreciate this small town like I should have. I can now. Walking around the perimeter to keep from blocking anyone's view, I find the people I am most looking forward to seeing.

"You were amazing!" Kirby takes a running leap and I catch her in my arms.

Mum and Fiona are sitting under the shade in their fold-up chairs with a spread laid out before them.

"Ye think so?" I ask her, nuzzling my face into her neck.

Christ, how does she smell so good? Like whisky and honey with a dash of paint from the house. It's my new favorite scent.

Intoxicating, really.

Kirby pulls back, the sun reflecting off her dark sunglasses. If only I could see her eyes. They'd be sparkling right about now. The way they do when she accomplishes anything at the inn, no matter how small.

"I mean, I've never seen bagpipers before and it all kind of sounds the same to me, but I thought it was beautiful. I loved every minute of you playing the bagpipes. Is that the right thing to say?"

I laugh, pulling back to tip her sunglasses up. "Close enough."

"You want me to play your pipes?" She waggles her eyebrows at me.

That has me laughing even harder. "You think you're so funny."

"Yes." She slides down out of my arms. "Hilarious."

"Cal. You were wonderful." Mum interrupts the two of us, coming up to us and giving me a hug. "I've missed ye playing in the games."

"Mum," I mutter, returning her hug.

"What? Cannae I say that?" She shrugs like it's no big deal. "Now, come eat. You must be famished."

Leave it to Mum to have the food ready to go. Not that I would turn it down.

Fiona is with her, raving about the parade into town. The four of us have an enjoyable morning, watching the different events go on around us while eating all the Scottish bakes my mum and Fiona made.

"What are these?" Kirby grabs another one of the

small balls sitting in the metal tin and dips it into the white sauce. "These are delicious."

"Do you really want to know, hen?" Mum asks. I love the sweet name she calls her. Like she's welcomed her into the fold without question.

"What?" Her gaze flies to mine, green eyes widening. "What are they? Is it weird?"

I smirk back at her, grabbing her hand then eating the treat straight from her hand. "Depends. Do you consider haggis weird?"

"That's haggis?"

I nod, chewing the bite in my mouth before grabbing another.

"Do you like it?" Mum asks her. "It's not for everyone."

"I love it." A blush creeps up Kirby's face. "I could eat the whole tin."

Mum grabs it back from her. "Now, now. These are for everyone. I'll show you how to make them."

"Really?" Kirby asks.

"Isnae that a family recipe?" Fiona asks, shocked.

"Nonsense." Mum waves her off. "Kirby can know the secret."

"Thank you, Miriam."

Kirby turns her eyes to the field to hide the tears welling in her eyes. I reach across and give her knee a squeeze. Her jaw tics, trying to hold in her emotion.

"You want to go grab a pint?" I stand. It's the only thing I can think of to try and help her.

"No need to hang out with us anymore." Mum waves us away. "Go. Have fun."

Kirby gives her a tight squeeze before standing.

"And be seen around town with you?" She's shaken off the earlier emotion. I think it's a good thing for her. I dinnae like seeing her upset for any reason, even if it's because me mum loves her.

"Aye. If that's okay with you."

Kirby wraps her arms around me and pulls me close. "And be with the best bagpiper in town? Hell, yes."

I laugh as I capture her lips in a kiss that's too sweet for my liking at the moment. If only we weren't still in the middle of town with everyone's eyes on us.

"I dinnae know if I'd go that far."

"Nope." Kirby shakes her head before grabbing her jacket and strutting off toward the main road. "I am the professional judge here of all bagpipers."

Running to catch up to her, I wrap an arm around her shoulders and walk us towards the pub. It's crowded with people who have already left the games and those who deem themselves too cool to hang out.

I used to be one of those people. I don't care now.

"Grab us a table and I'll get us a couple drinks."

"Okay."

I watch as Kirby finds an empty space at the end of a picnic table. It's weird because I never pictured myself being back here. Now, it's the only place I can imagine myself being.

With Kirby by my side.

I cannae wipe the smile off my face as I head to the bar and open a tab.

It's the perfect afternoon for people-watching and beers with Kirby. Henry and some of the boys from the band stop by and see us.

The pints go down more smoothly as the day goes on, and it brings out the flirtier side of Kirby. One I dinnae mind seeing.

"Come on. How many kilt jokes do you get in this?" Kirby's eyes are starting to glaze over. Whether it's from the fourth pint or getting up early, I'm not sure, but I grab her drink and down the rest of it.

It helps to cool the heat pooling in my veins at her hand sneaking up my thigh. I know she'll like what she finds there, but she's in no fit state for doing any of that tonight.

"Only from you." I wink at her.

"Smooth."

She rests her head on top of the picnic table and closes her eyes. Yeah, it's time to get her out of here.

"I'll get the tab." Henry gives me a knowing look. I've definitely played my hand and will have to answer all of his questions later.

Fuck it. I dinnae care. I dinnae care if everyone in town knows that I'm…what?

In like with Kirby? Fuck, that sounds mad. It's too early for love. Right?

Getting up, I lift Kirby into my arms and head out of the small outdoor area and walk toward our road.

I could easily drop her off at the lodge and head back to my own bed, but that's the last thing I want to do.

I've gotten used to the warmth and comfort of having her in bed with me every night. Her small body lines up with mine perfectly.

The lone light—that Kirby installed all on her own—by the front door is lit. Not that it's needed with the sun still shining brightly in the early evening sky. Shouldering open the door, I head straight for the stairs to take Kirby to her room.

"You're such a gentleman," she tells me around a yawn.

"Only for you, lass." I press a kiss to her forehead as I set her down on the bed and strip her out of her jeans, leaving her in only the oversize shirt she wore earlier.

She sinks into the bed immediately. Watching the way she curls up into a ball has me disrobing and joining her. Being the gentleman that I am, I throw on a pair of briefs that I kept here.

No afternoon delight.

"Mmm." She snuggles back against me, and I do my very best to ignore the growing feeling in my briefs. "I love…"

Before she finishes her words, she's out.

Fuck. What the hell was Kirby going to say? Love what?

Me?

This?

My cock?

It could be any number of things. Fuck. Maybe this is going better than I thought it was. My brain cannae process it right now, because just like Kirby, sleep pulls me under.

Chapter Sixteen

KIRBY

My head feels fuzzy. Darkness clings to every atom in my bedroom. There's a heavy weight resting over my side, and that's when I realize it's Callum.

More specifically, his arm. I have no idea what time it is. The last thing I remember was having a few beers at the pub with him and Henry. I don't remember getting *that* drunk, but day-drunk is exhausting in and of itself.

Behind me, Callum is snoring softly. I flip onto my back and look over at him. His hair is a mess and his mouth is open slightly. I feel like a creep just staring at him like this, but I can't help myself. Callum really is the sexiest man I've ever met.

Not wanting to wake him, I slip out from under his arm and find a pair of socks before heading off into the even darker house.

Something I'm still not quite used to.

Even in LA, there's a brightness to the night. So many city lights pollute the air. Here though? There's nothing. There's only one stoplight in town and that's it. The gas lamps dim at night, and it's not like we can see them from our piece of land on top of the hill.

I find that I'm liking it more and more though—the quiet and solitude that comes from being in a place that rests. That isn't always on the go.

I don't feel like I have to put on a face every time I step out of my house. Maybe that was part of my problem in LA. No matter where I was going, I was always portraying a different version of Kirby.

I never wanted anyone to see me as less than. It's probably why I was so focused on work that I didn't even realize someone was using my information to siphon money for themselves. Something I've been doing well not to think about these last few weeks, all thanks to Callum.

Instead of heading downstairs to one of the many ongoing projects, I head to the small door at the end of the hallway. Flipping on the light to the attic, I take the creaking stairs carefully. The last thing I want is to go falling through them.

I haven't been up to this part of the house yet. With so much to do downstairs, I figured this could wait.

Boxes upon boxes are stacked in neat piles against the walls. Dust is so thick in the air you can bat it away with your hand.

Trudging around old furniture, I stop in front of the first box. Antique, gold frames lean one against another.

Could this be my grandma?

A sepia-toned picture of a man and woman holding a baby in front of the inn is coming undone at the edges. There's more just like this one.

Christmas morning.

Summer holidays.

Vacations.

I can see them age before my eyes. As the photos get

newer, it's easy to see that the woman in the photos is my biological mother.

We have the same eyes. I must get my other features, like my wild hair and the quirk to my smile, from my father. A man I never knew, or cared to find.

I had no idea about any of this history. I never needed to. I had the best life growing up. My mom gave me everything I could ever want.

It's hard now to suppress all the questions that being here in Scotland is bringing up.

They looked happy. But a photo can only tell you so much.

My biological mother is no longer in the pictures now, and gone too are the smiles. Not long after that, it's only my grandmother in the pictures.

The sadness is too much, so I tuck them away and open one of the boxes on the other side of the attic. Old envelopes are tucked away here, and I pull out one of the letters.

Dear Clyde,

It's been a few weeks since Freya was born and we miss you dearly. I hate that work is keeping you from being here with us. This wee'un has your green eyes. The way she coos—I wish you could see it.

The neat scrawl goes on and on about the new baby in their lives. It has my breath catching in my throat as I try to make out the faded words on the old, yellowing paper.

Opening the box next to it, I find more of the same. There are boxes upon boxes of these letters, going back and forth. A newer looking box holds ones that look to have been returned.

Addressed to Freya in America. Los Angeles, to be exact.

Before I can open it, a creak from behind me has me jumping.

"What are ye doin' up here?" Callum's voice startles me and I drop the stacks of letters in my hands.

"Jesus, you scared me." I clutch at my chest, willing my heart rate to slow down. For someone as burly as he is, he sure does know how to sneak up on people.

A smile tugs at the corner of his mouth as he closes the distance between us. He's still in his boxers and looks drowsy with sleep.

"Didnae know where you went so late."

"What time is it?" I ask as Callum wraps an arm around my waist and pulls me into his hard chest.

"Half two."

"Sorry. I didn't mean to wake you."

Callum nuzzles his face into my neck, and it helps to calm the riot of emotions inside of me.

"What are these?" he asks, taking one of the envelopes from my hand.

"I'm not sure."

"Can I open it?"

"Sure." I shrug a shoulder and Callum sits back on the faded, maroon velvet chair.

I watch as his eyes flit over the words quickly before he hands it to me. "Looks like it was to yer mum."

I take the proffered paper from him and read it. From the sound of it, it looks like my mom ran off with a rock star to America, and my grandma wanted her to come home.

"Wow."

"Did you not know any of this?" Callum asks.

"No." I shake my head. "I didn't know about any of this until a few weeks ago."

Callum pats his thigh and I go to him, sitting on his lap. "How are you feelin'?"

The words on the page are a plea to come home. That she reacted badly and only wants to make things right.

"Am I going to find out that my dad was some famous rock star now?" I laugh, trying to ease some of the tension inside my chest.

"Would it make you feel better if he was?"

I wrap an arm around Callum's shoulders and lean into his hold. "Probably not. I never really needed to know who my biological parents were."

"Really?"

Callum's hand rubs steady circles on my exposed thigh, and it goes a long way in helping me feel better.

Just being in his arms is a balm to my soul. It's been a weird experience being up here reading about my family.

I run my fingers through his hair as he turns his ever-steady focus to me. "As far as I'm concerned, my adoptive mom is my real mom. I've been with her since I was two weeks old, and I never felt like I was missing anything in my life. But to know these people now? It feels…"

It's hard to get these words out. Callum doesn't push, just letting me take the time I need to try and vocalize it.

"It feels weird. Almost like I'm betraying my mom now by wanting to know more."

"Can you talk to her?" Callum asks. "Maybe she can help."

"Maybe."

Grasping my chin, Callum guides my gaze to his. The tender way he is looking at me has butterflies exploding in my chest.

"Anything *I* can do to help?"

Leaning closer, I capture his lips in a warm kiss. His hands drift up to my waist, resting there. Neither of us make a move to deepen it.

Feeling this connection to Callum goes a long way to settle me.

I've never felt like this with anyone before. Never had this need to seek someone out whose opinion I actually want.

I'm not sure how this cranky Scot wormed his way under my skin and into my heart, but he did.

"You're doing it just by being here." Pulling back, I rest my head on his shoulder and let him hold me.

His lips brush my forehead, and it has my butterflies sprouting butterflies.

"Glad my presence can help." There's a hint of amusement in his voice. "Maybe you can do something with all these letters."

"Yeah? Like what?" I close my eyes, more comfortable than I have any right to be in his arms.

"Frame 'em. Hang 'em around the inn. It's part of yer history, so why not display it?"

"Really?" That has me sitting up now and looking at him. "You think so?"

Callum brushes a stray lock of hair off my face and cups my cheek. "Why not? Everyone in town knows Lizzie, and I'm sure tourists would eat that shit up once you're running this place."

It has guilt settling low in my stomach. When I first started fixing this place, the end goal was to sell it. That hasn't changed. Callum's view on the lodge seems to have changed, though.

I don't want to disappoint him. Not when he has been one of the most important people in my life since getting here.

"You're right, they would." I do my best to sidestep his comment and ignore it. "That's a good idea."

"You know what's a good idea now?" he asks, squeezing me closer to him.

"What's that?"

"A shag and sleep."

"Callum!" Holding me close to him, he hoists me over his shoulder. The letters in my hand scatter across the floor. "We can't do that!"

"Says who?" Callum gives me a hearty slap on the ass that has me trying to cover my moan in his back.

"We have to be up in a few hours to get to work. The kitchen guy is coming to install the new countertops bright and early."

"Could always stay up all night…"

Callum takes the stairs down with ease, switching the lights off to the attic. The house is shrouded in darkness as he takes me to my room and throws me down on the bed.

"But then we'd be exhausted tomorrow."

Callum rests his hands on either side of my face, bending close.

"I keep hearing a lot of arguments, but I'm not seein' a problem if we're both satisfied."

"Mmm. Satisfied you say?" I throw my legs around his waist and pull him into me. He's already hard as a rock.

"Very much so, bonny lass. Many times if you'll allow it."

A wicked grin slides into place on my face. "Alright then. Satisfy me, Callum MacRae."

And satisfy he does.

Chapter Seventeen

CALLUM

"Aren't you supposed to be doing this, Mum?"

The spread of ingredients laid out before me is massive. I had no idea cooking involved this many…things.

"I have to take Thomas into town to pick up his car. I figure ye wouldn't mind helping Kirby."

There's a twinkle in her eye. From her, it means she's up to no good.

"Are you sure? I'm not the best chef."

Mum waves me off. "You can figure it out. Besides, you can read, right?"

"Is that supposed to be a dig?" I drop down into the small chair in the breakfast nook off the kitchen, sipping my coffee. "If it is, that means you didnae teach me."

"Ye numpty." She shakes her head at me as she dumps the rest of her own coffee into a travel mug. "If ye can read a recipe, ye can cook. Besides, I think Kirby will like you helping her much more than me."

"What's that supposed to mean?"

Mum comes over, dropping a kiss on the top of my head. "It means I notice ye sneaking in late at night. Ye've been spending all your time with her. I dinnae have to be a genius to know she would rather spend her time with you than me."

"Mum!" I shout at her, as she turns to leave the kitchen. "I don't need you poking around in my personal life."

"Ye've been married before, dear. It's not like I dinnae know what ye do. No point in hiding."

Christ. This is why I really need to get my own place. But until I know what in the world I want to do, is there really any point? With what limited money I do have, I dinnae want to blow it on a place I might not be in for more than six months.

"Mum. Just go and let me drown myself in my coffee."

She barks out a laugh at me. "Always a flair for the dramatics, Cal. Be a good boy and show Kirby how to make my haggis balls. Maybe she can make them for her guests at the lodge."

"Bye, Mum."

"Bye!" she chirps and is out the door, but she disnae get far. "Oh, Kirby. Lovely to see ye."

Ignoring my coffee, and the fact that I'm not wearing any shoes, I bolt outside right as Mum pulls her in for a hug.

"I'm leaving ye in good hands today," she tells Kirby.

"You mean you're not helping me?"

"That's what I said," I point out, not helpfully to my Mum.

"Ye'll both be fine. Just dinnae get *up* to anything. If ye ken what I mean." Mum waggles her fingers at us before getting into her car and leaving.

Kirby's mouth is hanging wide open. "Should I be worried about what she implied?"

I shake my head, the long strands of hair falling into my face. "I was told there's no need to sneak back inside."

"Lovely," Kirby tells me, sarcastically. "Always nice to know your partner's mom knows you're having sex."

I laugh before pulling her in for a kiss. Not that I didnae see her a few hours ago, but when Kirby is near, I cannae help myself.

The lass is just about the sweetest damn thing I've ever tasted. And if I can kiss her, I'm sure as fuck going to do it.

"Hi." She swoons into me. "If I could have been woken up like that this morning, I don't think we would have made it out of bed."

A smile twitches on my lips. "I can take you back there if you want."

"Show me how to make these haggis balls your mom keeps feeding me and then we'll see."

"Fine."

Steering her in front of me, I guide her inside.

"I've never been here before."

"What? Of course you have."

Kirby shakes her head, spinning in the kitchen. "You always come over to the inn."

"Well, this is the kitchen. I'm sure you've seen one before."

Kirby swats at my chest, but I catch her hand and dinnae let her go. "You're such an ass, Callum."

"You like it."

Rolling her eyes at me, Kirby leaves the small confines of the cozy kitchen, heading through the breakfast nook into the living room.

"Do you want a tour, or do you want to learn how to make haggis balls?"

Wide, hazel eyes are still taking in the small room that makes up the rest of the first floor of the cottage.

It's a small house, tucked into the side of the hill that faces the loch. It's been in the family for ages. All stone makes it cool in the summer and warm in the winter. The stairs sit in the back of the room, leading to two small bedrooms and one bathroom.

Having to share the tiny space with Mum isnae ideal, but we manage.

"Alright. Teach me your ways." Kirby giggles, and fuck if that isnae the sweetest sound.

"I hate to break it to you, lass, but we'll both be learning as we go."

"Really?" She follows me back into the kitchen. "You haven't made these before?"

I shake my head as I find the recipe sitting on the middle of the small, wooden counter. "Mum never really taught me how to make these."

"Great. You and your mom are going to have to move into the inn when we burn this place down."

"There will be no burning things down today, lass."

"Then let's get started."

Kirby rolls up her sleeves and takes the old recipe card from my hand. It's handwritten—hard to read in several places after years of use. "Is this a MacRae family recipe?"

"Mum likes to think so. I know a lot of people make them, but she says there's a secret ingredient in hers."

"And she's showing this to me?" Kirby clutches the card against her chest. "Am I allowed to be seeing this?"

I shrug a shoulder. "If she was concerned, she widnae have left the two of us on our own."

That earns me a laugh. "Then let's get started, Callum."

The recipe isnae that hard to follow. Mum laid everything out that we would need, so it's a matter of throwing the right amounts into the bowl.

It's not hard. As soon as everything is in the bowl, we're mixing it all together and getting it ready for the oven.

"Why dinnae we start with one batch and go from there."

"Okay."

Kirby wanders off into the living room as I set the timer. When I hear her gasp, I follow the sound and find her holding one of the picture frames.

Christ. I should've hidden these.

"This is you?" she asks, pointing to one of the small frames that sits on the mantel. "I can't imagine you like this."

"What, as a wee'un?"

The picture in question was from my very first Highland Games that me granda took me to. We're both dressed in kilts, and my smile is missing a few teeth. I remember that day. I couldn't have been more excited to be marching in the parade with him.

"Not as some burly man with all this hair." Kirby waves her hand over me. "You were so cute."

"Were?" I ask, closing the distance between us and boxing her in against the wall.

"Were." Kirby walks her fingers up my chest, igniting the lust that always seems to simmer just below the surface when she's near. "I don't think cute is appropriate for you now."

"What is?" I dip my mouth toward her ear and tug the lobe between my teeth. The groan it elicits has my cock taking notice.

"Attractive."

"Only attractive?"

Kirby's fingers dip lower, sliding under the waistband

of my sweats. The briefest contact has me thrusting into her touch.

"Hot. Rugged. Sexy."

"Mmm. That's more like it."

I dip my head down to take her lips in a steamy kiss. The tangle of her tongue as I slide mine against hers has lust curling through me. Dropping my hand low on her waist, I slide it into the band of her pants and pull her to me.

"Callum! We can't!" Kirby tries to push me off her, but puts little effort into it.

"Why not?"

"Your mom could come home any minute," she whispers, like she's been caught.

I shake my head, kissing a trail down along the throbbing vein in her neck. "She'll be gone for at least another hour."

"An hour?" It comes out as a purr.

"Aye." I give the globe of her arse a squeeze, rocking into her. Letting her feel my erection as it threatens to punch out of my pants.

"Then why don't you show me your room?"

Lifting the cheeky lass into my arms, I carry her up to my room, shutting the door and throwing her down onto the small bed.

Her eyes take in the room. It's nothing special. A few pictures sit on the bookshelf that Mum put in after I moved out and that's it. The dark navy bedspread is simple.

Based on the way Kirby is tugging me towards her and freeing my cock from its cloth prison, she disnae care about any of it.

Those plush lips of hers wrap around the head and…

fuck...me. The warmth and wetness has me thrusting into her mouth.

"Kirby. Fuckkkk," I groan out. When her hand snakes around me and starts tugging on my balls, I have to pull her off of me.

Her lips are swollen as I press my weight over her. Pushing her shirt off and over her head, I tug her bra below her breasts and devour the hard nipples. Kirby is a squirming mess beneath me as I lick and tug on the diamond tips.

"Callum. Please."

"Please what?" I pull off her with a wet pop.

"Fuck me."

"Anything, bonny lass."

Fishing around in the night table, I find a condom and make quick work of rolling it down my hard length. While I suit up, Kirby tugs her pants and underwear off and drops them onto the floor. Seeing this incredibly sexy woman laid out before me has me stroking my cock to try and stave off my own orgasm.

"Are you just going to stand there or are you going to fuck me?" Kirby asks, widening her legs. Her pussy is glistening, ready and waiting.

Settling over her, I push inside of her. "Fuck. Do you know how good you feel?" I give a tentative rock of my hips as Kirby grabs on to me. "So. Fucking. Good."

I puncture each word with a kiss as I start to thrust in and out of her. Her pussy squeezes my dick within an inch of his life.

"Harder, Callum. Harder."

"Aye, lass."

My moves get sloppier, messier, the faster I piston my hips. As we both drive towards the abyss of pleasure, our breaths mingle. Reaching between us, I strum her clit.

"Yes! Yes! Yes!" Kirby shouts as she comes, pulling my release out of me.

"Kirby!" I match her shout as I empty myself into the condom. "Fuck. Fuck!" I growl.

I collapse on top of her, both of us breathing hard. Kirby drags her fingers up and down the notches of my spine.

"Fucking incredible." I kiss the throbbing pulse in her neck. "So damn good."

"Aye."

I feel her entire body smile in that one word. But the afterglow doesn't last long. The smoke alarm blares from downstairs.

"Shit! The haggis balls!" Kirby shouts, grabbing her clothes and tossing mine at me. "Shit!

"Fuck."

Both of us run down the stairs as smoke fills the kitchen. Finding a tea towel, I open the oven door and pull the smoking things out.

"Oh my God!" Kirby exclaims, opening the window above the sink as I throw the pan in there to get rid of the smoke. "I can't believe we didn't hear the timer."

"Maybe if you weren't so loud…"

"Me? You're the one that was yelling!" Kirby slaps my chest.

Sweeping her into my arms, I nibble on her neck. "Do we need to reenact how that went down? I'd be willing to do so to prove you wrong, lass."

"You suck, Callum."

A cocky smile ticks up the corner of my mouth. "I believe that was you."

"Callum!"

"Now,"—I drop the bad batch in the trash—"care to try this cooking thing with me again?"

Kirby's eyes are sparkling as she nods towards the upper floor.

"If it ends like that, aye."

Chapter Eighteen

KIRBY

"There's really no updates?" I sigh into the phone.

"Sorry, Kirb. Nothing yet," Joanne tells me. "Not that they'd tell us anything. I think you're best just to lie low for a while longer."

"Believe me, that's what I'm doing."

It's going to be a gorgeous day here. The sunlight is peeking out over the tops of the trees, sending diamonds glittering across the surface of the loch.

The manor house is coming along. With almost the entire first floor done, it's time to start working on the rooms. Since the bedrooms aren't in the worst shape, I don't think it'll take that much longer.

Which has dread settling in the pit of my stomach. Once this place is done, what's keeping me here? The investigation should be wrapped up by the time I'm done, so why wouldn't I go home? My life is in LA, not this small Scottish town with one stoplight.

Right?

"Listen, I'm heading home—"

"Home?" I cut her off. "It's close to midnight there, isn't it?"

I glance at my watch, calculating the time difference with LA.

"There's a lot of work to be done since…well, you know."

"Since I was unceremoniously given the boot."

"Not yet," Joanne corrects. "This whole thing could still turn up nothing."

"It should since I didn't do anything!" I shout. I rub a frustrated hand over my forehead. This is not how I wanted to start the day. "Listen, I need to go, and you need to get home and get some sleep."

"Take care, Kirby, okay?"

"I will. Bye."

I end the call and drop my phone onto the brand-new countertop. I questioned Callum when he suggested it, but now I can't help but admire how good it looks in the space.

"Everything okay in here, lass?" Callum's voice startles me.

God, does he ever look sexy leaning against the doorjamb with sweats riding low on his hips. The shirt he's wearing is unbuttoned, exposing his six-pack.

"It's fine."

"Disnae sound fine." Callum pushes off the frame and walks over to me, caging me in. Pillow creases line his handsome face.

I shrug a shoulder. "Not much I can do right now about work."

"How about a distraction?" Resting a hand on my hip, Callum's warmth seeps into me. It settles all the errant thoughts rushing through my head.

"What kind of distraction?" I lean into his touch. I want more of it. Want to feel his warmth everywhere.

"Not that kind, lass." His breath is minty fresh. "I have a different kind of distraction in mind."

"What's that?" I ask, drifting my hands under his shirt and resting on the muscles of his back.

"Why dinnae you get cleaned up and I'll show you."

Pressing up onto my toes, I nip at his ear. "Care to get cleaned up with me?"

"Fuck. I can't say no to you."

Callum

"If I knew you'd agree this easily, I would have suggested this ages ago."

Kirby gives me a playful glare, her hazel eyes sparkling. "It's easy to say yes to you."

Holding out a hand, I help her down into the small rowboat. Even though it's a cloudy day, the temps are just right for a day on the loch.

"Then maybe I should think of a few more things that you could say aye to."

"Easy there, tiger." Kirby steadies herself as she drops down onto the wooden plank bench. It's nothing fancy. Just some boards nailed together. But I could never bring myself to get rid of it because my granda and I built it together.

The boat is small enough that Kirby's legs stretch out between mine. Using the oar to push off from the dock, I guide us out onto the water.

"Mmm. This is nice." Kirby's face is turned skyward, trying to soak in any warmth she can.

"I love being on the water."

"Really?" That has her peeking one eye open at me. "I don't think you've been out here since I met you."

I flick water at her as I dig the oars into the water and push us farther away from our small town.

"Ack! That is freezing!" Kirby throws her hands up, ready to block any more assaults if she needs to.

"I'd be out here more if it weren't for you."

"For me, huh?"

I nod, guiding the boat to a small nestle of trees on the opposite bank where we can float without being in the way of the tour boats. The ones that go out every day no matter the weather, carrying groups of tourists looking for the monster that lies beneath the surface.

"Debating paint colours—"

"You said you liked it!" She points a finger in my face.

"I do, aye. You're so easy."

"I hate you." Kirby laughs.

"No you don't."

"I'm debating." She gives me the side-eye before leaning back in the boat and turning her face skyward.

This Kirby is so different from the one when she first arrived. There was a tension to her that was evident to anyone that met her. She's more relaxed now. Easygoing. Maybe it's because we spend our nights wrapped up in each other, but this Kirby is someone I can see myself falling for.

Falling *hard* for.

"Did you know I've never been here before?" Kirby's voice is quiet. Boats are coming and going through the main part of the loch. We're left undisturbed here.

It's the perfect afternoon.

"Never?"

She shakes her head. "The only place I've ever been is

Mexico. Work was my life. I rarely took a vacation, and Mexico was because I got trips through work for good performance."

"Not that I ever went to Mexico, but I sent employees on trips for good work."

"Yeah?" Kirby peeks one eye open at me. "You've been quiet on what you do." She pokes one booted toe against my knee.

"It's not anything I'm proud of."

"As opposed to me that is under investigation for embezzlement?"

I snort laugh. "Guess we're more alike than I thought."

"What was it that you did, Callum?" Kirby asks again, leaning toward me.

Resting the oars in the locks, I lean back on my elbows, matching her pose. The sun is trying its damndest to peek out now with no such luck.

"I was in technology. Had one of the largest companies in the country. Made a living of buying out smaller companies to expand my own footprint. I was fucking brilliant at it."

"What happened?"

Drifting under the trees, it's cooler. A shiver racks Kirby's body and I shrug out of my coat and hand it to her. The smile she gives me has me telling her my story. Maybe this is why Kirby and I were so drawn to each other from the start. One workaholic recognizes another.

"I was a master at it. Knowing which companies could make us more money. Make me another million. It was easy when you have the brains for the business. But my ex-wife—"

"You were married?" Shock is the only way to describe Kirby's face as she burrows into my jacket. "Really?"

I nod. "Aye. She wasn't a nice person. Fuck, I wasn't a

nice person. I was all about status. Money. Making another million. Until…"

I scrub a rough hand over the back of my neck.

"Until what?" Kirby's warm hand lands on my forearm, giving it a squeeze.

Needing something to do, I grab the oars and start rowing us across the loch. There's the perfect spot for a picnic where I can take her. It helps to keep the emotions in check as I continue talking.

"She ran off with my accountant and all my money."

"She did what?" Kirby's jaw drops. The anger coming off her is palpable. It makes me fall a little bit harder for her, sensing the outrage on my behalf.

"Aye. I was a self-made billionaire before the age of thirty-five. After? I was left with nothing."

"Callum…I don't know what to say."

I don't look at her as I focus on the sound of the oars coasting over the water. "There's not much to say. I hired a forensic accountant, but he wisnae able to track it down. I sold my flat to support myself, but everything I worked for was gone. I dinnae know where the fuck they went, but if they ever come back here, they'll get jail time for sure."

It's not even the thing I'm least proud of. I save that. No need to make the woman detest me.

"I thought I had a rough go of it being investigated for embezzlement."

"Christ, we really are two peas in a pod."

The closer we get to the shore of the small picnic area, I let us drift until we bump into the shore.

"I'm so sorry they did that to you."

"I dinnae need your pity."

Kirby shakes her head. "It's not pity. I just don't know how anyone could do that to you."

"I wisnae a good person then. All I cared about was making money."

"It doesn't give them the right to do that."

Finding a wayward vine hanging from one of the trees, I grab it to steady us so we can hop out and have lunch.

"C'mon, out ye go."

I dinnae want to dwell on this. It's not something I like talking about.

Kirby steadies herself on my shoulder, but the vine snaps. It sends the boat rocking, and before I can find something to even us out, Kirby's arms go flailing, tipping the boat and sending us both into the icy water of the loch.

"Fuck!" Water drips from every crevice. It's ice cold. There's a reason I never swim in the loch and this is it. "Holy shit."

"Oh my God!" Kirby is bent over in two laughing, not a care in the world. "Not exactly the graceful exit I was planning on."

Being close to the shore, we're both able to stand. The small lunch is floating away from us.

Even covered in dirty water from the weeds drifting into the shores of the loch, Kirby is stunning. It clings to every part of her.

"Christ." I drag the branches off me, tossing them into the water. The boat floats into my shins, not going far. "Not exactly the afternoon I had in mind for the two of us."

"How about we head back to the house and see if we can start a fire in the fireplace?"

Extending my arm to Kirby, I help her back into the rowboat. It's too far for us to walk back and anchor the boat. With the wind blowing over the water, I'll need to move fast so we don't freeze our arses off.

"Best idea you've had all day."

Chapter Nineteen

CALLUM

"I'll be home tomorrow, Mum."

"No need to check in," she chirps over the phone.

I never felt the need to check in with her in the past. Hell, I barely called her more than once a month when I was living in Edinburgh. Seeing her every day now, it seems like the right thing to do.

Grabbing a bottle of whisky from the local distillery off the newly restored bar shelf, I head into the lounge to stoke the fire. The place is really starting to come together. Between Kirby's vision and our hard work, it might not take that much longer.

Which would be a damn shame. Because there is nothing I love more than tussling with her over paint colours and wallpaper samples.

"I know I huvnae been at home much lately."

"Ack. Ye think I mind? I'm glad ye're not moping around," Mum tells me. "I'm glad to see ye with a smile on yer face."

"I wasn't that bad."

"Says ye."

"Alright, Mum."

"Dinnae come home too early, son. Love you."

"Love you, Mum."

I end the call, shaking my head. Of course she would say that. Grabbing two lowball crystal glasses, I take the bottle and settle on the sofa in the lounge.

It's hard to believe how far this room has come along. Gone is the grimy and dirty space that this used to be.

The windows are sparkling, the lights from the town now easy to see. Photos hang on the green walls. With the wood panels on the bottom, it gives the room a cozy feel. The antique chandelier we found at a flea market fits perfectly in the room.

And with a fire now started? Tourists will love it.

Placing the glasses and whisky on the small wooden coffee table, I set another log in the fireplace and stoke the flame.

The floors above me creak, telling me that Kirby will be down any minute. I left her to get cleaned up after our second shower of the day.

Watching as the woman in question strides into the room, my jaw drops. In only my thick wool jumper and a pair of socks, Kirby is the most striking person I've ever seen.

"Warmed up yet, love?"

Kirby drops down on the sofa, burrowing into me. "I could use some of whatever is in that bottle."

Pouring a hearty splash in each of our glasses, I pass Kirby hers and clink my glass to hers. "Slàinte mhath."

"You know," Kirby says, sipping on her own drink, "you're going to have to teach me how to say that one of these days."

Sipping on my own drink, I keep Kirby close as the fire crackles. "You want a full-on Gaelic lesson?"

"Maybe." She tucks her feet under my thigh. The sweater fall just above her knees. "I feel like it'll help me fit into town."

"Lass, everyone here loves you."

Kirby sits up, pulling the jumper over her legs. "Some days it feels like I have no idea what I'm doing here."

"Yeah?" I ask her, tugging on a stray lock of wet hair.

"I mean, you haven't really made it a secret about how I have no clue what I'm doing around here." She waves a hand around the room, but I grab it to cut off this train of thought.

"Aye, but that's when you only just landed here."

"And now?"

I bring her hand to my mouth and press a kiss to it. Flipping it over, I press a kiss to the inside of her palm. The callouses there are from all the hard work she's been putting in.

"These hands have managed to change this entire room here. You did this, Kirby."

"With your help."

I shake my head, pulling her onto my lap. "It was your vision that brought this to life. Otherwise, it would've still been sitting here covered in grime with birds building nests in walls."

Kirby's eyes go soft. With the low light coming off the chandelier, it looks like gold laces the green. And the way they're looking at me? It's like it's bringing my heart back to life.

The damn thing hasnae felt anything for months, other than a fuck ton of self-loathing. With Kirby, it's like she zapped everything back into me that was missing.

"I'm just glad that you were here."

Swigging down the rest of my drink, I wince at the

burn. This is still one of the topics that I've treaded lightly on.

"I came home more out of guilt than anything."

"Guilt?" Kirby shifts back, resting more of her perfect arse on my thighs.

"There's more to the story." I rub my hands up and down her legs. Goose bumps break out over her skin. I love seeing the reaction I bring out in her—even if it might be the last time I see her like this.

"You mean your wife running off with your money didn't bring you back?"

"Ex-wife," I correct her. "And no. I had enough money from selling my flat to start over."

"Then what brought you here?"

"I was a fucking twat if there ever was one."

"Callum."

The way Kirby is looking at me makes me want to shut up and not tell her this. But if I want to have everything with her, I need to tell her *everything*. No matter how much of a bawbag I was.

"Money was the only thing I was concerned about. Buying out another company, to what, add to my millions? Mum called me and wanted me to come home for a visit. See my nan. But I couldn't be bothered. A deal was on the table that would have made me a hefty amount of pounds. Millions more. I was greedy for it."

Kirby doesn't say anything, just lets me tell this part of the story.

"I stayed. Didnae bother coming home, and by the end of the week, Mum called and my nan had died. It was sudden."

"Callum." Kirby's fingers cover her mouth, like she's trying to keep her emotions in check. Whether it's for me nan or me being a numpty, I don't know.

"I wish I were a better person and had chosen to come home, but I didnae. I came home for the funeral. By the time I got back to the city, my wife had run already run off with my accountant."

"I'm so sorry, Callum."

Kirby sifts her fingers through my hair, and the small contact helps to heal the still-open cracks in my heart.

I shake my head. "I don't want your pity. I don't deserve it."

"Callum. We all make mistakes. You couldn't have known what was going to happen."

The fire crackles behind us as Kirby traces her thumb over my lips in a tender way. Maybe I didnae scare her off with my selfishness.

"But—"

She shakes her head, dropping a lone finger over my lips. "I was so wrapped up in my own work that I didn't realize someone was stealing money under my account. You couldn't have known what they were going to do. What was going to happen to your nan. What matters now is that you're here now and being the person that people can count on."

I seal my lips over hers. This woman has been a balm to my tattered and weary soul. I didnae know what I needed to start healing. Apparently it was her.

Pulling back, Kirby nestles back into my side. She fits perfectly there. Like a piece that I didnae know was missing all these years.

"I've been a right piece of shite these last few months to everyone until recently."

"Oh yeah?" Kirby's breath ghosts over my chest. "What changed?"

I tell her the truth without any hesitation. Because I told her the worst part of me and she didnae flinch.

"You."

Chapter Twenty

CALLUM

"Wow. I cannae believe how different this looks."

Kirby's bright green eyes are assessing the almost completed kitchen. Over the last few weeks, her entire focus has moved into the dining room so the biggest part of the lodge is finished.

It's hard to believe how fast time is flying by with her. Days spent fixing this place up. Nights spent wrapped around each other.

I widnae trade it for anything.

New appliances. New countertops. New bar.

I had my doubts, but she proved them wrong. Seeing Kirby's vision is incredible.

The new island is made up of wood that was cut down from the trees that were infringing on the chicken coop. Different lengths of wood from the logs give it depth. The soapstone counter goes perfectly with the deep stain of the wood. The modern, stainless steel appliances give it the upgrade it needs to function as an inn.

Kirby spent more time than I would have sanding

down all the furniture in the breakfast nook and giving it a fresh coat of paint. Even if the chairs are mismatched, they fit in this room. Cozy enough for just over a dozen people.

With the windows freshly washed, you can see outside without the grimy build-up. Even if it is a dreich of a day.

"I told you it would come together." Kirby wraps her arms around me from behind. I love that we are constantly touching. Almost like we cannae get enough of one another.

"Aye. Shouldn't have doubted you."

"The floor guys will be here in a little bit. Got any plans as to what we can do for the next two days while they finish them?"

"Depends on what you mean by plans." I squeeze her hand with mine.

"You numpty," she says as she giggles. "Always thinking about sex."

This time, it's me spinning in her arms and lifting her onto one of the smaller tables in the breakfast nook. "Can you blame me?"

Kirby has one of my T-shirts on, tied up at the waist with a pair of jeans and a work shirt thrown over it. Her red hair is a mess of tangles floating around her head. If I hadn't overseen the electrical work, I would think she shocked herself.

Still, she's the sexiest woman I've ever met.

"We cannot spend two days in bed."

"Christ, lass. You're killing me." I bury my face in her neck and nip at the tender skin there.

"Callum!" She swats at me. "You did not just give me a hickey!"

"You didnae like my idea, so I had to do something."

Kirby shoves me away with a playful look in her eyes. "I had an idea if you're up for it."

I groan, trying to will my growing erection to soften. Anytime I'm around this woman, I get worked up. I always want to be touching her. Whether it's in bed or just having her in my arms, I'm addicted.

"Anything, lass."

"Want to head up to Edinburgh for the night with me?" There's a hopeful look in her eyes. One I don't want to crush. "There are a few shops I want to check out to get some things for this place."

The last time I was in the city, I had just come back from my nan's funeral and found out my ex took all my money and ran off. After that, I didnae want to be in the city. I didnae even bother grabbing what I needed from my flat before I sold it. I didnae want the reminders. Every memory from that place is tainted after my ex fucked me over.

But it's hard to say no to the woman in front of me. Maybe going and making some new memories might help. Erase the pain of the past.

As Mum would say, it's probably healthy for me. She'd even encourage it.

Fuck. I hate that she's now infiltrating my thoughts.

"On one condition," I tell her.

"What's that?"

"I do all the driving."

"YOU KNOW, you could teach me how to drive," Kirby tells me as she grabs my hand and pulls me across the street with her.

It was an easy drive here, one that I could do from memory. Kirby booked us a hotel for the night, so after dropping the car off, I'm following her lead.

"Lass, every time we come to a passing place, you screech like Mr. Peep."

"I do not!" she balks. "You drive like a bat out of hell."

"I dinnae know what that means, but you're wrong."

Kirby's not paying much attention to me as she leads us down the main road away from the castle behind us.

When she told me she wanted to come to the city for the day, I assumed she'd want to go see the big sights. Edinburgh Castle. Holyrood House.

Not at all. Everything in her sights is for the lodge. And I'd gladly follow her anywhere.

The skies are grey and lifeless, but thankfully it's not raining.

"Did you leave any room for fun in the agenda?" I ask her as we cross the street. Even though fall is leaving and the cold weather of winter is almost upon us, the city is still bustling with tourists.

"Did you have something in mind?" Kirby asks.

"You've tried haggis. How about black pudding?"

She winces. "Really? It's made with blood, Callum. Blood."

"Aye. It's a delicacy here."

She shudders as she glances down at her phone before turning us down another road. It's a road I huvnae been down. If it wasn't in the newer part of the city, I couldnae be bothered.

"Are you trying to scare me off, Callum? You should know by now, I don't scare so easy."

"Aye. I know better, lass. But if you want to be a true Scot, you have to try it."

Kirby stops in front of an old warehouse. It looks like it's seen better days. Much like the lodge we're fixing up.

"If I say yes, will you come inside with me?"

I have no idea where we are. She could be leading us into a cult, but based on the way she led us here, she knows what this place is.

"Aye. Lead the way, lass."

Chapter Twenty-One

KIRBY

"You know there's a perfectly good furniture store down the way," Callum tells me the second we step inside. A blast of warmth smacks us in the face.

I scoff. "I don't want everything to look like it was plucked out of an IKEA."

In searching for the kind of furniture I wanted for the lodge, I wanted to capture the history of Scotland. I didn't want anything mass produced, and this place was one of the top-rated stores to find what I have in mind.

The smell of mothballs hits me square in the face. It's packed to the brim—nothing but stuff from floor to ceiling, wall to wall. Paintings. Lamps. Bookends. I'm pretty sure I could find a real-life crown in here if I wanted to.

"It's not an IKEA," Callum tells me. "It's a modern furniture store."

I wrap my arms around his waist, pasting the sweetest smile I can muster onto my face. "But that's not what I want for *my* bed and breakfast."

"So I get no opinion."

I shake my head. "No. Especially if it's the wrong opinion."

"Can an opinion be wrong?" he asks.

"Yes. With you? The answer is always yes."

"Cheeky lass." Callum nips at my jaw, before dragging his lips up to my ear. "Can I get you to say yes to something else then?"

Shivers rack my body at the meaning in his words. For Callum, saying yes is easy. Whatever this man wants, I'll give him.

Wrong opinions and all.

"If you say yes now, I will say yes to anything you want to do later."

Callum pulls away, linking his hand with mine to pull me farther inside. A smile that is far too cocky graces his face. "Anything?"

"Within reason."

"Now there's limitations?"

"I will never go skydiving with you, Callum."

"Fuck no. That will never happen."

"Good. Then yes should be a reasonable accommodation."

Callum waggles his eyebrows at me. "Now, what in the hell are we looking for here?"

I shrug a shoulder, unzipping my coat as we head deeper into the long and narrow store. "I don't know."

"You don't know?" Callum sighs, exasperated with me. "I thought you knew what you wanted."

"No. I want to have a cozy feel. Old lamps. Antique tables. Things that people will see and think, 'oh, this is old time Scotland.'"

"How about this then?" Callum grabs the first thing in sight and holds it up to me.

Crossing my arms, I glare at him. "In what world

would I need a mini statue of a suit of armor in the lodge?"

"Scotland's history is riddled with knights. Dinnae you know this?"

"And you think that says welcome to Thistle Hill Lodge?"

"It's definitely unique."

The knight in question is tarnished at best. The steel of his suit is near black in some places, and the sword's tip is worn down. Instead of a knight in all his glory, he looks sad.

"If you want to buy him for your house, go right ahead."

Callum hmphs before putting him back. "Then you lead the way."

I chuckle as I pass him, trying to take everything in.

Floral vases. Old ceramic dishware. Tattered copies of books. Furniture that looks like it's within an inch of its useful life.

This little store tucked away in Edinburgh has a little bit of everything.

"This!" My eyes light up as I find an old crystal chandelier sitting on a dark, wooden table. From the gold arms, dozens of crystals hang off of it. "Can you imagine this in the foyer? It would look beautiful in there."

"Really?" Callum looks skeptical, as if he can't see my vision.

"Yes." I pick it up and give it a thorough once-over. "You'll see."

"I guess I will." Callum takes it from my arms and walks it over to the desk near the front of the store. He exchanges a few words with the older gentleman working there before making his way back to me.

"There are so many great things in here that will look great in the lodge."

"I'll take your word for it."

The barest hint of a smile is on his face.

I love this side of Callum. The one that he hides away from the world. It's like his beard is the mask he wears so he doesn't have to show people who he truly is.

He's not the hard man that doesn't want to be around people or help them.

No.

Callum is warm. The smiles that he shows me are small, but don't hide how he's really feeling. It makes me happy to know that I put them there. That I'm the reason he's smiling.

There's so much more to Callum MacRae than he shows the world. Even if I'm the only person to ever get to see it, I'll be happy.

"Lass. C'mere."

Callum breaks me out of my thoughts and beckons me to him.

"How about this?"

"Wow."

The piece in question is stunning. The half-moon table is weighed down with odds and ends that hide the true beauty of it.

The dark mahogany top has foliage carved into the edges that trails down and over the spiral legs of the table before tapering off to the feet.

"It's gorgeous." I run my hand over the dusty table, feeling its sturdy weight. "It'd be perfect—"

"In the entry," Callum finishes. "I know."

The fact that he can read my mind should scare me. That I'm so predictable that this man can read every thought I'm having.

It's not like I've made that a hardship for him though. When it comes to him, I'm an open book.

I don't even have to tell him I want it before he's waving at the old man and getting his attention.

There's a small card, detailing the history of the table, dating back to the 1800s. This is what I want to have in my bed and breakfast. Pieces like this. Ones that have history and meaning.

Even if my plan is still to sell it, I want everything to be ready for the new owner so that all they have to do is list the rooms and it'll be open for visitors.

To know that I left my stamp on a small part of something even if I'm not there.

I don't know why that thought has my heart twisting in my chest.

The plan was never to stay here. It's not like this is my house. It never was. So why do I keep thinking of it like that? Why is the thought of someone else running it doing funny things to my insides?

"Okay, lass. All squared away."

And this man. He isn't mine to keep. No matter how much I want him. It has my stomach falling to my feet.

I try to push every negative thought out of my head. I want to enjoy the time I have left here. I don't want to waste a second of my time with Callum.

"Thanks for coming with me." I squeeze him to me.

"Like I said, I'll always say yes to you."

"Then how about we head back to our hotel?"

"Want to make a quick side trip?" Callum asks, cupping my cheek.

"Yes."

The answering smirk on his face is enough to have me rethink every one of my plans. Because being in Callum's bubble might just be the only place I want to be.

Chapter Twenty-Two

CALLUM

My nerves are a tangled, jumbled mess. After arranging payment and delivery of the items Kirby found at the antique store, my brain decided it was a good idea to show Kirby where I lived.

Why? I have no fucking clue.

But those wide eyes of hers were looking up at me with so much emotion, I couldnae stop the words from spilling out of my mouth.

The antique store, situated near the main part of town, is only a short walk to the newer part of Edinburgh.

Where the brick monstrosity that I lived in sits.

"This is where I used to live." I point to the building in question.

"Really?" Kirby's tone carries a hint of doubt.

"Aye. Very top floor." I point to the top floor where my old flat was. The front of the lobby is nothing but floor-to-ceiling windows. Every corner of the building has a balcony looking onto a different view of the city. With the penthouse, I got every view. It was wildly over the top. Even with the cloudy skies, there's a bright glare coming off the front windows, like the residents are sequestered away and not to be ogled by others.

Some days I'm ashamed that I used to be this person. The only remnant of this life is the money I made from selling this place.

"It's…"

"Terrible?" I finish for her. "Ugly? An eyesore?"

Kirby shakes her head. "Not you."

"Trust me, this is the person I am."

Even when I was married, I didnae spend much time here. Not that she cared. She was happy to spend the money I made us. It kept her happy, so I was fine.

"Is that how you see yourself?" Kirby spins to stand in front of me, moving up one of the steps so she's eye level with me.

"I'm not a good person. I know that now."

"Then. You weren't a good person then, Callum." Kirby drapes her arms over my shoulders. "But that isn't who you are now."

"And who am I now?" I wrap my arms around her waist and pull her flush to me. Her face lines up perfectly with mine, our foreheads kissing.

"You're Callum MacRae, the best damn son and person anyone in the town of Aberlach could have ever hoped to have. You help people without even thinking about it."

"Even if Mum made me?" I interject.

Kirby smiles, wide and happy, at me. "You would've helped me without her. Besides, you did all that work to help Fiona with the Highland games."

"It was the right thing to do. She's old."

"Fiona would kick your ass if she heard you say that." Kirby laughs. "But you did it because even though you think you're this terrible person who did everything for money, you're not. Under all this burliness there's a kind heart that you're afraid to show the world."

"I am?"

"You are. You're a good man, Callum. And even if you might not see it, everyone else does."

I slant my mouth over Kirby's, cutting off any further comments. After what she said, I cannae help but want to kiss her. To shut off the turmoil of emotions that she set off in my head.

I did my best to shut down any thoughts about my life here when I moved back home. It was easier in my quest to heal. Turns out, I wasn't healing. Not really.

Cutting open these old wounds, I realize I never gave myself the space to deal with them and move on.

Kirby made it easier to do. To cut myself open and dump everything at her feet. When she didnae turn away from me, I realized how fucking lucky I was.

She's goodness wrapped in a fiery ball of sass. I only hope she disnae realize how much better she is than I am.

"I don't think the people here appreciated you," Kirby tells me. "I think they used you, and they couldn't see how wonderful you are, or they would have never fucked you over like they did."

"Maybe." I sigh.

"Except…"

"Except what, lass?"

"If they didn't screw you over like they did, I wouldn't have met you."

"What if I was back home and just happened to stumble upon you?"

Kirby quirks a brow at me, sliding her nails through the hairs at the nape of my neck. "You said it yourself. You never went home. I doubt that would've happened."

"I cannae say that I'm pleased those twats ran off with most of my money, but I am glad you landed up here."

"Me too."

I dinnae know if the person I was here was ever the real me. It's a persona I projected to the world to try and make a living here.

The me now—living in Aberlach and helping people? This me feels like the real me. The version I was always meant to be.

Not making millions upon millions of pounds. Not running a company to solely buy out smaller ones and drive them out of business.

But this version. Me helping out in town where needed. Helping Kirby with her house. Nights out with friends. Taking Kirby out.

This feels more like the real me. The one I want to be. Because the man I was in Edinburgh never would've made time for friends and family.

Even if my ex and accountant get the justice coming to them, would it change things now? Would I pack up and come back here?

Doubtful.

"This seems like an entirely different life," I confess to Kirby.

"Would you come back here if you could?"

"C'mon. Let's walk. I don't want to stay here."

Putting some distance between me and the place that seemed to suck my soul from me helps to clear the fog clouding my brain.

"Honestly? If you had asked me a few months ago, I would have. But now?"

Kirby squeezes my hand as we come to a stop near the Scott Monument. The castle looms large behind it, with an eclectic mix of people coming and going.

"Aberlach is where you want to be?"

Looking down at her, I nod. "Maybe not still living with Mum, but aye."

Kirby tries to hide her smile but does a terrible job of it as the light changes and we cross the street. "Don't worry, I'm not judging you for living at home. Hell, I moved out of my place before I came here and stayed with my mom."

"We're more alike than I ever thought."

"I guess so. Is there anything else you want to do here before we leave?" Kirby asks. "Any other places you want to show me?"

I shake my head. "Is there anything *you* want to do? I've seen it all."

"I wouldn't be opposed to you feeding me. Taking me out on a real date."

"A real date? I've taken you out, lass."

"Mmm, have you?"

Finding a bench that sits on the outskirts of the park in the shadow of the castle, I stop Kirby and pull her down. "What about the day at the loch?"

"But was that a date?" Those green eyes of hers are sparkling with humour. "You picking me up and taking me out to dinner. I want to be wined and dined, Callum."

Grabbing her legs, I pull them up and over my lap. A cold wind has picked up and I want all the warmth I can get right now. "Are you saying I huvnae won you over?"

"Will it get you to take me out?" Kirby pulls me in closer by the lapels of my jacket. I love how easy to read she is. She's still joking around, and it helps to lighten the heaviness of the earlier mood.

I don't like what this place stirs up inside me, so it's easy to escape into Kirby.

Sure, I might not have asked her out or made it official,

but it doesn't mean our times together huvnae felt like dates to me.

If I'm not with her, I want to be with her. When I am with her, I cannae stop touching her. It's like my body craves her with a need I've never felt in my life before.

What Kirby wants, Kirby gets. And if that requires me asking her out on a real date, so be it. Because I'll do anything to keep that gorgeous smile on her face for as long as possible.

"Kirby Stewart. Would you like to go on a proper date when we get back to Aberlach? Where I pick you up and take you to dinner?"

A smile lights up her face. "I thought you'd never ask."

Chapter Twenty-Three

KIRBY

I wish I wasn't so nervous. It's not like I haven't gone on dates before. But it's been awhile. A *long* while. Longer than I care to admit.

All because I wanted that damn VP position.

Except, how did that turn out?

It makes me wish I had friends here so I could talk to them about this. Talk through these nerves with someone.

I drag the straightener through my hair, and it falls perfectly for once in my life.

Thank God. Because I'm going out on a date. With Callum.

A *real fucking* date.

Callum was rather shifty on the details.

I pull the green, cable-knit sweater over my head and look at myself in the mirror. The sweater brings out the green in my eyes. The skinny jeans cling to my legs, showing them off. Stepping into my warm boots completes the outfit.

Hopefully it will drive Callum crazy.

With too much time to wait and wonder how this could play out, I grab my phone and call Joanne.

It rings and rings before sending me to voicemail. Huh. She always picks up my calls, no matter how mundane my reason for calling. It sets off a niggling feeling in my brain.

But it's not something I need to worry about now. Instead, I dial the one person I know I can count on.

"Kirby, sweetheart. I haven't heard from you in a few days." Mom's voice rings out loud and chipper. "How is everything?"

"Good. Everything is good here."

"How's the house coming along?"

"Well, it's coming. We've got the kitchen almost done."

"We? Who's we?"

Grabbing my perfume, I give myself a spritz before dropping into the chair sitting in my room. It's really turned out nice, though it's one of the only bedrooms upstairs that is ready.

"I told you about the guy who's helping me," I tell her.

"You did not!" Mom scoffs.

Oh crap, I could have sworn I told her about Callum. Hell, there's been so much going on here that I've barely had any time to breathe, let alone think.

This might turn into a much longer conversation than I wanted to have right now.

"He's my neighbor."

"Your neighbor. And he's helping you with the house."

"That's about it."

"That's it? Kirby. I need more details than that. I'm your mother."

"What do you want to know?"

If we were on a video chat, I could see her eye roll. I don't know what it is, but I can always feel it, even if I can't see it.

"He's a big, burly guy who knows how to wield a sledgehammer." Sarcasm laces my tone.

"Knows how to wield a sledgehammer? Oh, Kirby."

"What?"

Pushing up and out of my seat, I head down the stairs and look around for Callum's overwhelming presence. It's not like I wouldn't have heard him if he came in. The front door squeaks like a bitch every time someone opens it.

"This is the first time you've ever brought up a man to me."

"This is not the first time I've talked about a man to you."

"Sweetheart, for the last ten or so years, it was all about school and then work. And now this manor house. So yes, I would recall if you'd ever mentioned a man to me."

God damn my mother and her mind that remembers everything.

"Well, he's helping me because I couldn't do it by myself. YouTube will only get you so far."

"I tried to tell you that you should have hired a contractor and done it from afar."

"Well, as you know," I point out to her yet again, "it's not like I had anything better to do with my time."

"Well, is he cute?" she asks, ignoring my comment.

"I mean, more or less."

"More or less? That must mean he's drop-dead gorgeous."

"Mom!" I laugh.

"What? You're not giving me anything. I need to try and figure this out for myself."

This is the thing with being an only child to a single mother. She's my best friend and I've always told her everything. Mom was there for my first crush. My first boyfriend. My first real heartbreak. She's been there for everything and wiped my tears away.

Of course she would now want all the details about Callum. Details that I'm wary to give because what's going to happen in a few weeks when I leave?

Sure, Callum and I have this thing going now. But this isn't my life. My life is in LA, not here.

"He's a nice guy, Mom. A little opinionated on the house that he has no claim to, but there's not a whole lot to tell you."

"Oh, my dear." Mom laughs. "I will get these details out of you one way or another."

I laugh. "And on that note, I have to go."

"Go where? Is he taking you to dinner?"

"Goodbye, Mother. I love you."

"Love you, Kirby. Don't forget to call and tell me all about your date. Bye!"

I end the call, shaking my head at her. Even though she wanted to know all about Callum, it helped to push my nerves to the side.

Standing in the lounge, I can see him walking up the drive, hands fidgeting in his coat pockets. Even from here, his beard looks tidy. The long locks of his hair are swept back into that ever present bun. Dark jeans mold to his legs, and the top of a grey sweater peeks out from behind his coat.

In a word? Sexy.

Grabbing my own coat from the small coat closet—one of the few rooms that only needed a good dusting—I slide into it before opening the front door.

"Holy shit." Callum's breath comes out around him in a fog. The cold has finally taken hold here, clinging to everything. "You look fucking gorgeous."

Grabbing the sides of his coat, I pull him toward me

and give him the sweetest of kisses. I can't help myself. Callum MacRae is irresistible.

"Not so bad yourself."

Blue eyes sparkle down at me as his fingertips ghost over my skin. The softest touch has heat spreading through me.

"You ready?" Callum's voice comes out laced with desire. It hints at things to come for later tonight.

"Let's go."

Taking my hand in his, Callum leads the way down the lane. The old gas lamps are starting to pop on as darkness settles over the town.

A few families are getting treats from the ice cream parlor as the shops that are still open start closing down for the night.

Callum stops in front of the lone hotel that sits on one side of Main Street. It's like something out of a Shakespeare play. With sand-colored stone lining the lower floors, the tops are painted white with flower boxes resting in each dormer window.

"Hope you don't mind." Callum opens the door to the restaurant connected to the hotel. "There's live music tonight."

"Sounds perfect," I tell him.

It's one of the few places I haven't been in town. It smells of cheap beer as we step into the warmth of the hopping restaurant. Faded-red, worn carpet covers the floors. Old wooden panels cover the bottom half of the walls while the rest is painted red to match the floors.

Fake candles sit in sconces flickering on the walls. Booths and tables fill the space, packed to the brim with people.

"Callum. You're finally here," the host says by way of greeting. "I had to fend people off your table."

"Cheers, lass." He drops a kiss on her cheek as he passes and slips her a twenty-pound note. I follow Callum to a small table that sits under the window with a "reserved" sign sitting on the dark wood top.

The stage is directly in front of us, next to the bar. "You want a pint?" he asks.

"Please."

I don't hide my ogling of him as he strides to the bar in a few short steps. It seems like everyone in town is here tonight as Callum sidles his way to the bar. He's greeted with a smile, but someone cuts off my delicious view.

"Kirby. How are ye?" Fiona asks, dropping into the empty seat. "We don't see ye out often."

"I've got that big old house to take care of."

"I hear from Miriam that ye're doing a fine job."

"That's awfully sweet of her. It's coming along."

"Fiona," Callum interrupts, dropping both ice-cold glasses down onto cardboard coasters. "Nice to see you."

Her eyes grow wide as she takes in Callum's towering form. "Are ye here together?" She wags her finger between the two of us.

"We are." I grab the drink sitting in front of me and take a long pull of the lager.

"Well, I'll be." Fiona's eyes shift to Callum. "I guess ye don't need old Mary now, do ye?"

"Be kind to Mary, Fiona. But that was always yer plan, not mine." Callum shoots a wink in my direction.

"This is a date then?" Her gaze flirts between the two of ours. Callum is staring down at me with a coy smile on his face. I love that he's getting easier and easier to read.

"I'll let you two be." She presses up on her toes and drops a peck on Callum's cheek. "Be sure to come to the bakery tomorrow, aye?"

"Aye."

Callum takes his seat, taking a long drag of his drink.

"And who might this Mary be?" I rest my elbow on the table and lean over to him.

"Christ, I knew you'd pick up on that." Callum scrubs a hand down his face. "Isnae it impolite to talk about other women on a date?"

"Well, now that Fiona has brought it up, I want to know about this."

Callum shakes his head. "She disnae know when to not say things. She might be a bigger gossip than my mother."

"Were you really questioning that? I don't know her that well, but she always seems to be gossiping with someone."

"I think it's why she runs the bakery," he tells me matter-of-factly. "She always wants to be in the know. People come in for sweets, then they give her the scoop on their lives."

"So she's paid in gossip then?" My eyes twinkle as I stare at Callum over my drink. The noise level in the bar rises as the band takes the stage. They start tuning their instruments as stragglers come in, bringing the cold with them.

"Aren't you funny, lass?"

"I try." I take a sip of my beer, watching as Thomas from the hardware store walks over.

"I heard you two were in town tonight."

"For fuck's sake," Callum mutters under his breath.

"Hi, Thomas. How are you doing tonight?" He's one of the few people in town that I know very well. Anytime I have questions on what I'm doing, he never minds helping me find the solution.

"Oh, just fine. Had to make the trip into town tonight to see the band."

"It seems everyone is here," I tell him.

He's dressed nicer than usual in finely pressed brown pants and a heavy sweater with a tartan collar sticking out around his neck. Freshly shaven, it almost looks as if he's here on a date too.

"Have you heard them play before?" Thomas asks.

"I haven't. Have you?" I bring Callum into the conversation.

"Once or twice." Callum's answer is short.

The band seems to have finished warming up, and the first chords reverberate through the bar.

"I guess I better get back to my table." Thomas waves two hands at us. "Just wanted to see ye both."

"Nice seeing you, Thomas."

"Jesus. Fiona probably called everyone in town to let them know we're out together tonight."

I bark out a laugh. "She probably did. Does that bother you?"

"I'm used to them by now." Callum tips his drink in my direction. "They're equally as invested in your life now, too, lass."

"Me? I'm only a newbie here. No one really cares about me that much."

"Do you think they'd be coming over to talk to me if I was here by myself?"

"Well, Fiona would. Because she has to set you up with Mary."

"Are we back on that?" Callum groans as the band plays around us. It's a catchy tune, something that has a Gaelic sound to it. I love it, even if I don't know at all what they're singing about.

"You never told me who she was."

"Someone I went to school with."

"And you didn't want to date her?"

"Why would I date her when I can have a sassy redhead?"

"She might be too much for you."

"You're telling me."

Except a smile lights up Callum's face, evident even in the low lighting of the restaurant. I hide my matching one behind my beer as couples start to crowd the dance floor.

"Dance with me, Callum." I set my beer down and hold my hand out to him. He looks at it like I'm crazy.

"Nae."

"Oh, come on. I want to dance."

Pushing up from the table, I move to stand in front of the burly man whose eyes are now focused on me.

"I'm a shite dancer."

"Don't care. I'll probably make you look better, because as you say, I'm a right shit dancer too."

"Christ, are you really gonna make me do this?"

"Yes," I say with a nod. "I'm not taking no for an answer."

Bending over, I take his hands in mine, but lean over to whisper in his ear, "Trust me, I'll make it worth your while, Callum."

"You know just the right things to say to get me to do whatever you want, don't you, lass?"

"I do."

"And this is a power you're not going to stop wielding against me?"

"Nope. I'm glad we have this settled."

Callum stands, linking hands with me as I walk us backward toward the small dance floor. No one here is going to be winning any awards. People are having fun and don't seem to care what they look like.

Dropping my hands onto his hips, I try my best to get

him to loosen up, but the stoic look on his face has laughter billowing out of me.

God, these are the kind of nights that I'll always remember. The ridiculous dancing in a small-town inn in Scotland. The look on Callum's face as he shakes his hips in an awkward manner on the dance floor. The smiles from the other people out here that I know.

Long after I leave and put Aberlach behind me, I'll remember this.

The smile etched across Callum's face does funny things to my insides as he twirls me around and pulls me into him.

"You're really not a good dancer, lass."

"You're not much better than I am." I laugh.

Callum spins me again and we start our own version of a swing dance, tapping our feet together as best we can.

Everyone's laughing or clapping along to the band before a slow song comes on. Callum immediately drops my hands, but I don't let him get far.

"Don't think I'm letting you get away that quickly."

He groans as the dance floor empties out, though a few couples are still holding on to each other. The ballad is Gaelic, and I don't recognize a single word, but I don't have to. Not when Callum takes me into his arms.

"Do you know what they're singing about?" Callum asks, pressing his lips to my ear. There's a graveness to his tone. I dig my fingers into his biceps as I hold on to him.

"No."

"They're singing about being in love. About the heartache that comes with it when the one you love leaves."

"Is it really a love song then?" My head sits just under his chin as I whisper against his neck. The throbbing of his pulse has me pressing my lips there.

"It's about an old love returning to where they found their home. To a place where they feel like they can belong. Finding new love."

I let Callum's words wash over me as I think about the meaning of them. It's almost exactly how I'm feeling right now.

This place that I never even knew about is slowly becoming a part of me. I never really thought about that happening when I came here. It was just going to be a temporary stop on the road to getting what I've always wanted.

But maybe the love song is right.

One thing ends and brings up a new beginning. I didn't plan on finding a place that would mean so much to me.

On finding Callum.

I can't love him, can I?

There's no way.

Callum tips my chin up for me to look him in the eyes. Eyes that are full of emotion and glittering as the song ends.

"Thanks for the dance, lass," he tells me before taking a sweet kiss.

Callum doesn't linger, but I don't let him pull away. I need the anchor of his mouth to keep my head sane right now. The things this man is doing to me—swirling everything around and turning it to mush.

What was supposed to be a fun night out started toying with my emotions. Has me thinking about things that I have no right to think about.

Like a future here in Aberlach. With Callum.

Damn these love songs for making you feel all the things.

Chapter Twenty-Four

CALLUM

Kirby has been quiet. Ever since that damn slow dance, she's been sipping on her drink and swept away in her thoughts. No matter how much I've tried to bring her out of it, all I got was a smile before she turned her focus back to the band.

With the music ending for the night, I close out our tab and grab Kirby to walk her home.

"Everything okay, lass?" I ask as soon as we're outside.

The streetlamps are still shining bright. There's a bite to the air now, nipping at our cheeks as we set a brisk pace back to the inn.

"Savoring the night is all."

Kirby wraps an arm around my hips and snuggles in close. Pressing a kiss to the crown of her head, I relish her warmth and try not to push it.

"So, Callum. How is this date going to end?" Her voice cuts through the quiet of the night.

"How would you like it to end?"

There's a smile threatening to take hold on my lips. It's not something I've done much of—at least not until recently. I was a grumpy asshole before I met Kirby. Now, she's lightened that load on me.

Coming to the gates of the inn—the newly fixed gates, by yours truly—she spins away from me, chewing on her bottom lip. "I was hoping you would come home with me."

Closing the short distance between us, I lift her into my arms. "Then we're on the same page."

"Good thing." Kirby's lips are warm as they kiss a path down my jaw, tugging my earlobe between her teeth.

"Fuck. That feels amazing."

Every nibble, every suck, has my cock growing harder in my pants as I shoulder open the front door and kick it closed behind me. I don't have the good sense to take her up to the bedroom.

No. The need coursing through my veins is too powerful. Like it might explode out of me if I dinnae get my hands all over her bare skin.

Dropping her arse on the small table that now decorates the entryway—the one we found in Edinburgh—I pull her jumper off and toss it behind me.

Her breasts are straining against the material of her bra as I drag a finger over the swell of them. Watching the goosepimples break out there has a growl tumbling out of me.

I love seeing how turned on I make her. The blatant need shining in her eyes has me leaning down and covering her satin-clad nipple with my mouth.

I'm not gentle as I bite down on it. Kirby's hands are raking through my hair, making a right mess of it as the slightest bit of pain stings with each pull.

"Callum. That feels amazing."

I glance up at her, finding her eyes closed and her teeth biting into her bottom lip. I lick a path over to her other breast and give it the same attention. This time, more teasing. More soft licks. Gentle nibbles. Warm breath blowing over the tight bud through the wet material.

"You're driving me crazy," Kirby whines.

I smile against her chest as I press open-mouth kisses up to her neck. "I like seeing how turned on you get at my hands."

"I'm not feeling those hands."

"You mean these?"

Slowly, painstakingly slowly, I drag my hands up the soft curves of her stomach, resting just under her bra. My thumbs skate over the soft material there, not quite giving her what she wants.

"Ergh. More."

"Patience, lass."

I take my time.

Untying each boot and tossing them behind me.

Every article of clothing is meticulously removed, thrown into the growing pile at my feet until she's left only in her underwear.

Stepping back, I drink in my fill of this woman. I only had one beer tonight. Not enough to even get buzzed.

But the feeling of seeing Kirby drunk on lust in front of me? It fills my veins and clouds my head.

All that bare, ivory skin waiting to be devoured at my touch. The nipples, diamond hard, begging to be plucked.

Undoing the button and zipper on my own jeans, I free my cock from his denim prison. He's aching to get inside Kirby.

"You think this table can withstand a good fucking?" I give myself a slow stroke.

"Think you can fix it if it doesn't?"

A blush creeps up Kirby's chest, likely from the thought of me fucking her so hard, the table breaks.

Challenge accepted.

Fishing a condom out of my wallet, I drop it onto the table before falling to my knees in front of her.

I throw her legs over my shoulders as I drag my tongue through her folds. She's wet. Dripping with need.

The taste of Kirby on my tongue is so sweet. I'll never get tired of it. I take my time, licking and sucking on her, devoting attention to the tight bundle of nerves that drives her crazy. Strumming my tongue over her clit has her grasping my bun and grinding down on my face.

"That's it, bonny lass. Fucking come."

I attack her pussy with renewed fervor, trying to keep my own release at bay. There's no way I'm coming anywhere other than inside Kirby.

"Callum!" Hearing Kirby shout my name about damn tips me over the edge, but I squeeze my cock to keep it from happening. Feeling her wetness on my lips is heavenly.

Sitting back on my heels, I'm eye level with that sweet pussy. I drag a finger through it, wanting to touch her. Wanting to drag out her orgasm before I slam inside her.

"Holy shit," Kirby whispers. "So good, Callum. So fucking good."

Kissing her inner thighs, I stand and grab the condom. The sound of the wrapper has Kirby sitting up and taking it from my hands. Her small hands roll it down my hard length, and shit…her touch has me ready to thrust inside her.

"You ready to test out this table?" I ask, brushing her hair out of her face.

"Do your worst." Kirby smirks.

Lining myself up with her, I push inside in one long, hard thrust. There's instant relief at being surrounded by her warmth. Kirby's arse is at the edge of the table as I hold on to her waist to give myself the leverage I need to piston my hips.

I'm not gentle. After the weirdness at the end of the date, I need this. The relief to clear my head. To not worry about how she's feeling. To please her.

"Fuck." I go faster. Harder. My touch is bruising as Kirby drags her fingers down my chest. "Fuck, Kirby."

Sweat clings to her brow as she pulls me closer. Her heels are digging into my arse, urging me on.

"I'm so close."

"God. You feel fucking amazing. The way you're choking my cock. Fucking incredible."

I heap praise on her as I pepper her skin with kisses.

"Oh! Oh, I'm…I'm—"

Kirby cannae finish her sentence as she explodes around me.

"Yessss," I hiss. It only takes a few more thrusts before I'm emptying my release into the condom. "So fucking good."

"Callum." Kirby's voice is a purr. "That was incredible."

"I'd give it an eight."

"What?" she shrieks.

"Next time, I'm going to fuck you so hard we break this table."

"Deal."

Kirby laughs, and I love that this is how the two of us are together. Every time with Kirby is better than the last. But this time? Something about it feels different. It's still fucking explosive as ever, but there's something else. More emotion? More tenderness?

I don't know what it is, but I'm savouring this moment. Tattooing every gasp and moan into my skin. The way her fingers are clutching me to her, like she might float away without me.

I want this. Want everything this woman will give. She hasn't been shy about her plans of selling this place and leaving town. But maybe, just maybe I can figure out a way for her to stay.

Chapter Twenty-Five

KIRBY

"What do you mean it won't be in? It was supposed to be here yesterday." I rub a hand over my forehead, trying to stave off the impending headache.

It seems like nothing is going my way right now. Instead of working on getting the bedrooms ready and finished, I'm still waiting for four queen beds. And the beds that are ready—the small singles—have no bedding, all because of a delay with the shipper.

If only I didn't feel the need to make this place unique. If I had gone with more modern furniture and patterns, it would've been fine.

I should be able to handle this. Hell, it's what I did for a living. But without having access to shipping manifests, it does me no good.

"The shipment should be here in a fortnight," the person on the other end of the line tells me. "End of month at the latest."

"End of the month? That's two fortnights! I can't be waiting on this for four weeks!" I cry.

"I can't make it arrive any faster."

"There are no other options? A different warehouse maybe?"

I smack my head against the wall behind the check-in desk. Another thing that needs to be done. With so much going in and out, I didn't want to get this finished and risk it getting damaged, as evidenced by the chunk taken out of the corner from a wayward tub going in.

"Sorry, lass. That's all we've got. You want a very specific pattern, aye? And that will take a while to get here."

"Fine. Thanks for your help."

"Aye."

He hangs up before I can get another word in edgewise. As if the delayed furniture isn't bad enough, a drop of water lands smack-dab in the middle of my forehead.

Looking up at the ceiling, there's a slow drip coming from the upstairs. I know the king's suite—as I dubbed our fanciest room—is there. It's the one we've been staying in while we get everything else ready.

Fuck me.

Rushing upstairs, I open the door to the bathroom to find Callum in the shower. Instead of taking a minute to appreciate him in all his naked glory, I shut the water off.

"What the fuck?" he shouts, soap dripping down into his eyes.

"The shower is leaking."

"Leaking? Leaking where?"

I toss a towel to him as he wipes the soap from his eyes and wraps it around his waist. Okay, maybe there is a second or two to appreciate how fine he looks with water sluicing down his abs. When he asked me to join him in the shower this morning, I said no because I had too much work to get done.

A list that seems to be never-ending right now.

"Downstairs. I felt it when I was on the phone."

"Christ. I'll take a look," Callum tells me, stepping out of the shower and turning the sink on to rinse the remaining soap from his hair.

"Shouldn't we call a plumber?" I ask him, leaning against the doorjamb.

"I can do it." Callum shakes his hair out before pulling it back from his face and tying it into a messy bun.

My eyes lock with his in the mirror. "I know you did it the first time, but something isn't right. We need a professional."

His brows furrow ever so slightly in annoyance. "It's probably a loose screw somewhere. It should be an easy fix."

"Then why don't we get a professional to tell us that then?" I cross my arms as Callum turns to face me, leaning against the bathroom counter.

"Are you doubting my abilities, lass?"

"I just want it done right!" I shout. With things not working out like I had planned, I need one thing to go right today.

And things not going right is something I'm not used to. At work, if something wasn't scheduled correctly, or there was a hangup at a port, I could pick up the phone, make a few calls, and get it taken care of.

Here? Here, if it's not arriving on time, there's nothing I can do. If something in the house breaks, I don't know the first thing about fixing it.

I was hoping by now I'd have more news about what's going on at home, but it's been crickets. Joanne hasn't picked up the phone in a week or two, and it has my nerves on edge. Now with another setback here, all I want is to get this house done and sell it.

"What's wrong?" Callum asks, grasping my elbow.

"And dinnae say nothing because obviously something is wrong."

Pulling out of his hold, I pace the room that has become my sanctuary from the chaos of the house. I don't know why I thought it'd be a good idea to live in the same space we were renovating, but I didn't want to be holed up in a hotel for God knew how long.

"The shower is leaking, Callum. On top of it not working, I now have to figure out how to repair the ceiling and ensure there is no water damage. I don't know how much that is going to cost, but having to rip open the ceiling and fix it? Not something I wanted to deal with this morning." My voice grows louder the more I talk, but I'm on a roll, so watch out. "Plus, some of the beds won't be here for a few more weeks, and the beds that are here have no bedding. So what's the point of opening a bed and breakfast if there are no beds?! Hmm? No point at all."

My chest is heaving as I pace in front of the windows. They're fogged up from the cold morning, hiding the view of the loch beyond.

"Is that everything?" Callum asks.

"No. Because if I can't figure out how to deal with these issues, what business do I have even fixing this place up? I should know how to do this. But I don't. And I hate feeling like an idiot." I blow out a breath. "Now I'm done," I whisper.

Callum pulls on a pair of boxers and drops the towel before walking over to me. "Deep breaths, lass."

The warmth from his hands, still hot from the shower, seeps into me and helps to calm all the racing feelings inside of me. I do as he asks, letting everything he's telling me sink in.

"I'll call the plumber as soon as I get dressed. We'll do

some research to see if we can find the beds anywhere else. And as for running this place?"

"I said fixing it up," I correct him. "I'm still selling it."

"You are?" That has him dropping his hands from my shoulders.

The look in his eyes guts me. I haven't hidden my intentions about selling. It felt unfair to lead him on. From the minute I met him, I told him that was my goal.

To see this look of shock on his face that I don't plan on keeping the lodge adds more weight to my already heavy shoulders.

"I don't have the first clue on how to run an inn. I can barely manage this as it is." I wave a hand around, indicating the house around me.

"Right. Well, I guess we better figure out the issues and move on. If you dinnae have the beds, the new owner can always find some."

Callum grabs the shirt that lies across the end of the bed and pulls it on over his head.

"Callum."

"It's fine, lass. Better get started on the day's work, aye?"

He doesn't look back as I listen to him head downstairs.

One more thing that I've somehow managed to fuck up today. God, can one thing go right?

The last thing I want to do is hurt Callum, but he has to know that I don't plan on staying here.

As much as I've loved every minute I've spent with him, my life is in LA. I'm hoping that once the investigation is complete, I'll have the promotion I've always wanted and have job security for life.

Running a B&B in Scotland was never on the list. With the changing of the seasons, there's no way I would be able to withstand the ebbs and flows of a business that depends on tourists.

I want security. Doesn't everyone?

Maybe if I explain all of this to Callum, he'll understand. Hell, he knows just about as well as anyone how easily things can be taken from you.

As soon as my foot hits the top step, the lights flicker before everything goes dark. I hear Callum grumbling from the kitchen.

Fuck me.

Can one thing go right today?

Chapter Twenty-Six

CALLUM

It's been a weird few days. Trying to fix things around the house hasnae been easy. The leak in the shower is going to take more time to fix than we originally hoped. Having to dig into the tile is never an easy job. When the plumber broke this news to us, I could see the tension grow in Kirby's face.

It was a setback she didnae want to deal with.

I get it. I do. But isnae this the kind of thing that happens when working on houses? It's not the end of the world. But it's made Kirby hyperfocused on everything else in the house.

If there is a spot of paint that disnae look right or something she has now decided disnae fit, we have to go back and fix it.

It's because of this that I'm spending my morning fixing the wood shelves in the lounge. Kirby decided she didnae like the stain colour she originally chose, so she's having me redo them.

I didnae want to add to the stress lines that keep cropping up between her brows. So I put on the best smile I could muster and got to work.

All this after spending the night in my own bed. Kirby said she was too worried to think about anything but going to sleep last night. I didnae want to push the matter, so I spent the first night at home in a long time.

It's probably why I feel so off this morning. Ever since we started this thing together, we've spent our nights wrapped up in each other. Hell, our mornings too. Kirby isnae one to hide how she's feeling, so it's weird.

I wish the lass would open up to me, but every time I try to bring it up, she brushes me off. I thought we were well past this now, but I guess not.

And through it all, I've been trying to figure out a way to ask her to stay. Because now that I've had a taste of her, I dinnae want anything less than her.

She's it for me. But with the way she's carrying on about paint, I dinnae know if she'll be open to hearing it.

Like I said, it's been a weird few days.

"Do you think that's looking better?" Kirby asks, coming up behind me. "Or is the original better?"

Fuck.

"There's only so many stain colours, lass."

"But—"

"Kirby," I cut her off, "whether you do the lighter or darker, the bar shelves look good."

"But—"

I drop the paintbrush down on the small towel I set on the bar and turn to face the woman that is going to make me crazy today.

"Why the need to change the stain? It looks fine."

Her eyes widen and nostrils flare. Fuck. It was exactly the wrong thing to say as I wait for her to explode.

"Fine? Do you think I'm going for fine?" Her words are eerily calm.

"No, but—"

"Fine isn't the look I'm going for, Callum." She spits my name out like she's pissed off at me—which she most definitely is. Sure, we bickered when she first got here, but that was for fun. This time? Kirby is actually mad.

I wave a hand over the bar shelves. "Kirb, lass. This colour now? It goes with the bar top. Both of them go with the room. Why are you worried about this?"

"Because, Callum. I want everything to pop. It needs to look perfect. I don't want to drop the ball."

"You know that everything going wrong isnae because of you, right?"

"I'm in charge though."

Placing my hands on her shoulders, I smile as her head drops into my chest. "Deep breaths, lass. I promise, these things going wrong arnae because of you. It happens."

I rub my hands up and down her arms as I feel the tension start to drain out of her.

"Sorry. I know I'm not making things easy for you."

"Aye, it's okay," I tell her. "Let's take the day off, lass."

"Callum. We can't. There's too much work to do."

"A few hours isnae going to hurt. I think you could use it." Kirby looks like she wants to say something but disnae. I can see her weighing the decision. Before, she widnae have hesitated to say yes. She's now debating if she can afford a few hours away with everything going on. "Let's go grab breakfast at Fiona's, aye?"

That has a small smile tugging at her lips. "A quick buttery and coffee?"

"That's it." I kiss her. "And after that, we'll be back here to finish up these shelves and get back to work."

Kirby rests her head on my chest, looking at the shelves behind us. "I guess we can keep them the same colour."

"Oh no. I'm halfway done. There's no going back now."

"Sorry. I don't know why this place is turning me into this person. I'm not usually like this."

"Things like this can make anyone a little mad." I pull back, cupping her cheek and turning her to face me. "But instead of barking out orders, why dinnae you talk to me about it?"

"I wasn't *barking* out orders," Kirby huffs.

Dropping a finger over her lips, I shush her. "I think I'll decide who is doing the barking of orders around here. And it was you, lass."

"I—"

"No." I shake my head. "You went a little mad, and we're going to go get a buttery and some coffee to help settle all these thoughts in your head."

"And how do you know that I'm having all these thoughts?" she mutters against my finger.

"You're easy to read."

"Am not."

"Whatever you say." I turn her and push her towards the stairs. "Now, grab your shoes and let's get some breakfast."

"Fine."

Kirby winks at me before bounding up the stairs. It was a simple enough gesture, but it let me know she was feeling a little more relaxed.

It might be a small thing, but at least I can help her, even if she's been frosty towards me the last few days. Maybe there's something else she isnae telling me. Maybe she heard back about the job? I dinnae know. All I know is I'll be there for her.

Whether she wants me to be or not.

Chapter Twenty-Seven

KIRBY

"You ready to get to work, lass?"

Callum steps behind me, caging me in by the counter. Two cups of coffee are waiting to be drunk. He burrows his mouth in my neck.

"I guess. Although, I'd much rather be back in bed with you."

"Maybe after we finish the check-in desk."

Callum's warmth and strength surround me. I could get used to this and to waking up every morning next to this man. Hell, I'm already used to it.

Callum and I have spent every spare minute of our time together. I've had to learn to let go of things I can't control, like the shipping issues. It's let me enjoy the time I'm spending with Callum without worry. If we're not working on the house together, we're in town. Having dinner with his mom. Getting breakfast at Fiona's. Walking along the loch.

I never imagined I would enjoy a life like this, but I love it. I love the slower pace of life. Waking up without having to rush off to a meeting after staying at the office well past a respectable time.

"I need to go grab some clean clothes from home, lass."

"Okay."

"Be back in a minute." He gives me one last kiss before reaching for his coffee.

I hide my smile in my mug as I watch Callum leave the kitchen. It's hard to believe how far this place has come since I got here.

The entire dining area is going to be the jewel of the Thistle Hill Lodge. With views of the loch, anyone who visits will fall in love here.

We haven't been eating in here, but it's ready for guests. The tiny vases of thistle that sit on each table give it the perfect finishing touch.

A buzzing in my pocket pulls my thoughts back to reality. An unknown LA number rings through onto my phone. Something in my gut tells me not to ignore it.

Swiping on the call, I lift the phone to my ear. "This is Kirby."

"Kirby. Beth in HR at Thompson. How are you?"

"Beth. I'm shocked to hear from you."

"Well, I have some good news for you."

"Good news?" I ask, not wanting to get my hopes up. "What kind of good news?"

"Well, we've finished our investigation into the money stolen from the accounts."

"Okay." I walk around the counter and drop into one of the refinished chairs. There's a spot on the wooden table that I trace with my finger. "Are you able to tell me what you found out?"

"We'd like for you to come to the office on Monday and discuss what we learned."

"Monday? As in four days from now?"

It's a good thing I'm sitting, because otherwise I would've been knocked off my feet. Monday? There's no way I can make it back in time.

"Yes. The investigators from the FBI will be in the office and will discuss everything then. Your presence is needed."

"Not required?"

"Well, I don't want to say it, but yes, it is required."

"Okay. Monday."

"Will that be a problem?" Beth asks.

"No. No problem."

I can't find any words. This is what I wanted, right? It's like the first day I arrived here. I couldn't string more than two words together because things kept going on.

Exhaustion.

Nearly crashing my car.

Exploding toilets.

Now, I'm trying to figure out how to breathe because the moment I've waited for is here.

In LA. More than five thousand miles from where I am now.

Callum chooses now to come back inside. He's not paying attention, fishing around in a bag from Fiona's that Miriam probably picked up. When his eyes snap up to meet mine, the smile that was sitting there falls from his face.

Shit.

"We'll discuss all the logistics of it then."

"Okay. That's fine. I'll see you then." I end the call without another word.

The sick feeling in my stomach swells.

"Everything okay?"

He drops down in front of me, hands landing on my

knees. Instead of making me feel better like his touch always does, it only makes the feeling in my gut grow.

"That was the office."

"And?"

"They need me back there on Monday?" It comes out as more of a question.

"Do they?"

"Yes."

My mouth is suddenly dry and I can't force the words out. "I need to be there to wrap up the investigation."

"And?"

I can't have this conversation with Callum so close. It's messing with my brain. And my emotions. "They said it was good news, so my guess is I'll be cleared."

"So that's it?"

I nod, standing, as his hands drop away from me.

"My life is in LA. I need to get back there."

"We still have work to do here."

We. This place is mine, but Callum has never, not once, shied away from the hard work it took to fix it up. I couldn't have done it without him. It feels wrong to be making this decision now without him, but what choice do I have?

"Callum…"

"Are you really just going to leave this place behind half-finished?" Callum asks, turning to face me.

"What can I do? I have to be there."

"Fuck them. They gave you the boot without doing their due diligence."

"It's not like I can just ignore it, Callum! I have to be there."

"That's it? You're just going to pack up and put this place in your rearview mirror?"

"This was never permanent, Callum. I was always planning on leaving."

Even if it feels like my heart is cracking in my chest.

"After everything we've been through? You're gone. You dinnae care about who you're leaving behind?"

"Callum."

"It's fine. Whatever."

Callum turns to leave, but I don't let him get far. Grabbing his bicep, I turn him to face me. "That's all you're going to say to me?"

My voice wobbles, emotion getting the better of me.

The man in front of me is not smiling. His gorgeous face is devoid of any emotion. It has my heart sinking further.

This isn't the man I've come to know and love.

God, do I really love him? How in the world am I supposed to leave right now when I'm just realizing this?

Or maybe you were lying to yourself.

Callum shrugs. "You're leaving. Your life isnae here. What else is there to say? No point in dragging this out."

"Ouch."

A lone tear escapes, much to my dismay. I brush it away with too much force.

"Would anything I say make you want to stay here? You're the one that's always had one foot out the door." There's an angry set to his shoulders. They're bunched up by his ears as he scrubs an angry hand over his face.

"That's not fair."

"Isn't it though?" Callum throws at me. "Just a way to pass the time while you're here before leaving?"

"Well, if it really meant so little to you, then you shouldn't care that I'm leaving." The lie feels bitter on my lips as I spit it out. "Guess there isn't anything to stay for."

"Guess not."

Callum gives me a hard once-over before storming out of the inn. What tentative grip I had on my emotions snaps when I hear the door slam shut behind me.

What started as a promising day of working in the house I've come to claim as my own took a turn I wasn't expecting.

Is this everything I wanted to happen? Did I want my name to be cleared? Yes. I didn't do what they accused me of doing. But…is that job still what I want?

Angus wanders by on the road, pulling a watery laugh from me. I'm sure he's looking for food.

He's just one of the many things I'll miss about this place.

I drag myself upstairs to the chaos that has become my life here. Packing the little I brought with me, I decide it's time to pull on my big girl panties and get my life back.

Even if what Callum said wasn't true, it still hurts. None of this was just a way to pass the time. I didn't mean to fall in love with this place. Or him. But it happened anyway.

Is it all part of the bigger picture? A way to realize that when I get back to LA, I need to have more in my life than just work?

The rain starts to spatter against the bay windows in my room, and for once, it's a welcome sight. I give in to the tears as I hastily pack my bag.

There's no point in staying here any longer than I need to. It'll only hurt more.

I guess LA is finally calling me home.

Chapter Twenty-Eight

KIRBY

"Are you ready for your meeting today, Kirby?" Mom asks me as I fasten another bobby pin into the low bun at the nape of my neck. It took more effort than I care to admit to get my hair into a somewhat presentable state. The last however many months, all I've done is throw it into a messy bun and call it a day.

I haven't cared enough to do anything.

Hell, I never had to put on a front when I was with Callum. He didn't care what I looked like.

"I don't know, Mom."

"Aren't you going to feel vindicated when you meet with them?"

"I don't know."

"Well, it has to feel good because they're calling you back in—"

"Mom!" I snap. "I said I don't know."

Mom clasps her hands in her lap as she sits on my bed, a knowing look on her face.

When I left for Scotland, I packed up everything in my

apartment and brought it here. With no end in sight, I figured getting rid of my apartment would be better than keeping it. And now as I'm in my childhood bedroom getting ready for this meeting, I can't think straight. Can't put more than two coherent thoughts together.

"Something's bothering you."

I sigh. Of course, my mother's intuition is dead on. Not that it would take much to get to the bottom of why I'm in a mood.

"Well, I don't really know what I want today."

"Then why'd you come back?" Mom asks.

"Because my life is here!" I snap.

I rub a hand over my forehead. I have no idea how I'm going to get through the day if I can't keep my emotions in check. Especially since I'm snapping at my mom when she didn't do anything.

"Sorry. I'm still jet-lagged and angry."

Angry that I'm here in the first place.

Angry that I got pulled away from Scotland.

Angry that I didn't wake up next to Callum this morning.

How did this even happen?

How did I fall for the burly Scot who met me when I was covered in toilet water? It tugs a smile from the corner of my lips.

"See, now you're happy," Mom oh-so-helpfully points out.

I don't roll my eyes at her, but walk over and drop down onto the bed and rest my head in her lap.

"I don't know if I'm making the right decision being here today."

"Did you have much of a choice?" she asks, brushing a stray lock of hair behind my ear.

"No?" I ask more as a question than a statement. "I

don't know what's going to happen today. I don't know if I'm going to have a job. I don't know if I'm going to be arrested. God, I just don't know."

"What do you want then? And if you say I don't know, I'm going to smack you."

I smother a laugh at my mother's words. Of course, that would get her going.

Well, what do I want?

My emotions are one big, jumbled ball since I got on the plane. The minute I landed in Scotland, everything felt off. Nothing felt right. I was supposed to be here in LA and not in some small town in the Scottish Highlands.

And now being here in LA? Nothing feels right. It's that exact same feeling.

"What if this isn't what I'm supposed to be doing with my life?" I ask my mom.

She peers down at me with deep brown eyes, as if she's trying to look into my soul.

"The few times I talked to you on the phone, dear, I'd never heard you sound happier in your life."

"Really?" I ask. I pick out a hangnail on my finger, trying not to let my emotions overwhelm me right now.

"Really?" she parrots back at me. "Yes, you've always been driven and wanted to succeed and move forward with your life, but at a shipping logistics company? Is that really what you want?" She quirks a brow down at me.

A choked out laugh comes. It's more like a sob than anything.

"It's the only place that gave me a job after college. Why wouldn't I want it?"

"Kirby, honey, you're not the same person you were eight years ago."

Hell, I'm not the same person I was five years ago. Hell, even five weeks ago.

"For once you seem happy. There's laugh lines on your face."

I swat at her arm. "Are you telling me I'm getting old?"

"No, it means you're happy, dear. Something I don't think I've seen from you in a long time. Genuine happiness."

"But…" I stutter. "My life is here with you."

"Kirby, I'm your mother. I will always be your mother, no matter what. Whether it's here, whether it's in Scotland, whether you decide to flit off to Thailand and train elephants—whatever you want to do—I will be your mother, wherever you are in the world. Whether you're a VP at a shipping company, whether you own a manor house in Scotland, I'll be there for you. I'm always a phone call away. Now, put on your big girl pants, go to this meeting, and then decide what you want to do with your life."

"I love you, Mom." My laugh comes out watery.

"I love you too, dear. Now, go figure out what your future holds."

WALKING into the all glass building, my nerves are a riot. My emotions are all over the place. The last time I was here, I was unceremoniously kicked out.

Is this what's going to happen again?

Am I going to leave in handcuffs?

I have no idea what's going to happen today, but I won't know unless I go inside.

Like my mom said, I need to put on my big girl pants and do this.

The minute I step into the lobby, I'm greeted by Ross.

"Kirby, I'm glad you're here today."

He doesn't show a lot of emotion, but I'm trying to get

The Highland Escape

a read on how he's feeling. He's not flanked by cops, so that has to be a good thing, right?

"It's nice to see you again," I say, shaking his proffered hand. "It's been a while."

"Yes, it has," he confirms. "And hopefully there'll be some good things we can talk about today if you want to follow me upstairs."

Right, because I don't have my badge.

I was stripped of everything when I left that day, and it should put a sour taste in my mouth at how I was treated.

But honestly, it's hard to feel much of anything right now.

Being that it's midday, the elevator isn't as busy as it usually is, and we take the car up to the fourteenth floor in silence.

I keep my hands folded in front of me, trying to keep the nerves at bay. Fidgeting won't do anybody any good right now. When the elevator doors open, the HR director is standing there to meet us.

"Kirby."

Short and sweet is the way this is going to go.

"Hi, Beth."

"If you'll follow me."

I trail behind her as we head toward the conference room. Curious eyes are popping up from behind cubicle walls as I pass. I'm like a fish on display for everyone.

What are they going to see?

My eyes travel their own familiar path, looking for Joanne, but not finding her. I texted her to meet before this morning, but with getting in so late, I never heard back from her.

Now, not seeing her at the office? That unsettled feeling is coming back full force. A few people smile at me as I walk by, but I can't manage more than a weak smile in return as I head into the conference room. Two men in finely pressed black suits, if not a little too big for them, are waiting for us. They look official, almost like they could be FBI.

Are these the ones that are going to arrest me? They said it was good news, so that doesn't seem likely.

Christ. I have no idea what's going on.

Callum. I'm saying things he would say, and it has my heart dropping out of my chest. This is not where I'm supposed to be right now. I wonder what Mr. Peep is up to. If anyone left his shows on for him.

"Kirby, please have a seat." He indicates to the men behind him. "We worked with the FBI while you were gone to uncover what's been going on."

"Okay."

The leather chair is uncomfortable as I reach for the water pitcher to pour myself a glass. I take one big gulp, trying to wet my mouth because it's suddenly as dry as the Sahara.

"Miss Stewart."

"Please, call me Kirby," I tell them.

"Okay, Kirby." The older man with salt and pepper hair addresses me. "As you are aware, you've been the subject of an investigation at Thompson & Associates."

"I'm aware."

"As standard with any investigation, we had to revoke all of your access to the system in case you were the culprit behind the theft."

"Were?" That sounds promising.

"After a thorough investigation, it appears that someone was able to hack your login and do everything in your name."

I keep the retort to myself. I already knew this.

"As you can see,"—a stack of papers is pushed in my

direction—"based on the timestamps, you can see your logins."

Pulling the stack toward me, all the numbers blend together. Is this really what I did for the last eight years? Looking at numbers to try and make companies more money than anyone could possibly need?

This is the last thing I want to do.

That thought hits me like a train. I've never felt so positive about something in my entire life. Being here in this conference room, it's not what matters anymore.

What matters is Scotland.

What matters is Mr. Peep. And Angus.

Callum.

God, I miss him. The easy cadence of his voice that soothes every part of me. The way he holds me. Smiles at me.

How could I have left him like I did?

What an idiot, I chide myself.

"Kirby?"

"Sorry. What was that?"

"Would you like to know what happened?"

"Yes."

"Because we've made an arrest, we're able to disclose that it was Joanne."

"Joanne?" My jaw hits the floor. "Like Joanne *Joanne*? But why would she do this?"

They can't be serious. I've known Joanne for years. There's no way she would do something like this to me.

"We have already arrested her and filed charges, but from what we were able to glean, she got greedy. Said something about being jealous that you were getting the promotion and raise."

"She really said that?"

Beth nods. "Against her attorney's better judgment, yes.

We left your accounts open just in case someone would try and make a move. And she did."

I'm stunned. "I guess I'm in shock she did this."

Joanne. The person who was my confidante while I worked here all these years. I can't believe she would try and set me up like this.

Holy shit.

It's like I came back home and all good vocabulary was sucked from my brain.

"Did she say why she needed the money?"

Ross shakes his head. "She didn't. We've reviewed all internal accounts, and it looks like you weren't the only person she targeted."

"Wow."

"We're sorry, Kirby," Ross tells me. "We wish this never happened, but you can understand we had to do our due diligence of investigating."

Beth pushes over another stack of papers. "That promotion you're wanting. Vice President? It's yours."

"Is this so I don't sue?" I ask, taking the letter off the top, seeing a hell of a lot of zeros on their offer. That amount of money would set me up for the rest of my life.

But what kind of life would it be if all I'm doing is working?

The old Kirby would have jumped on this. In one perfectly crisp piece of white paper, everything I've always wanted is laid out before me.

So why am I hesitating?

Because I don't want it. The new Kirby doesn't want anything to do with this. The new Kirby wants to buy the first plane ticket back to Scotland and run into the arms of Callum.

"So Joanne is in jail and I'm off scot-free?"

"More or less," the second FBI agent confirms.

"More or less?"

"More details will most certainly come to light as part of the ongoing investigation to see if there's more money hidden in accounts we couldn't access. But there will not be any record against you, and your files have been wiped clear of any wrongdoing."

"Wow." I sink back into the chair and cross one leg over the other.

When I came in today, I put on my best pencil skirt and jacket, almost as a suit of armor to prepare myself and guard against anything that could happen.

It's not my work boots and oversized jumper that smells like Callum.

"Do I have time to think about this?"

"What is there to think about? Isn't this what you've always wanted?" Ross asks.

Clasping my hands, I lean forward and address him directly. "Ross, this was exactly what I wanted when I walked into this conference room all those weeks ago. Then I got shown the boot, and what happened instead was I found myself. I realized this isn't what I want from my life."

God, this is the most real thing that I've ever said to anybody and I'm telling it to my boss.

Ex-boss now. "Ross, I don't want this job. I don't want to sit cloistered away for fourteen hours a day making companies more money when I could be having a life."

"Is it work-life balance you're worried about? We can make sure you're out of the office every day by seven," Beth interjects.

"That's just it though," I tell her. "Our clients are all over the world. There is no nine to five workday for me. My days are always come and go, and I never know what it's going to bring."

Not that running a Scottish inn is going to bring the same thing every day.

"What do you want then? More money? A different position? Name it, Kirby, it's yours."

"What I want, you can't give me." I push the papers back toward them and stand. "Effective immediately, I resign from Thompson and Associates. You'll understand me not giving my two-weeks' notice."

They look at me like I've grown another head. Just like that, I'm done. The only real job I've ever known is over. As I walk out of the conference room, my mind is still spinning.

Joanne did this. She set me up and for what? More money? She was a good employee. We both got paid a good salary. And then, what, Joanne got greedy and stole from clients and set me up? I still can't believe it.

I hate that I let myself get set up like this. I don't look at anyone as I take the same path I've walked for years. I want to get out of this place. It's like it's closing in on me and I can't breathe.

My watch beeps at me, a text from my mom and more words of encouragement. I don't think I've ever lived more than ten miles from her. Hell, the farthest I've ever been from her was in college, and even that was in the same city.

I don't know what life is going to look like, but all I know is that life is in Scotland.

As I wait for the elevator to take me down, I pull my phone out of my purse and start looking for flights. Now that I've made up my mind, nothing is going to stop me from getting my life back.

My *real* life.

All I want is my inn.

My cow. Even that damn rooster that loves cooking shows.

And Callum.

For once in my life, I'm not making a calculated move. I'm flying by the seat of my pants and going after everything that I never knew I wanted.

Scotland and Callum.

Chapter Twenty-Nine

CALLUM

"Cal, how much longer are ye gonna be in here?"

Mum's voice calls out to me from the lounge. It echoes around the empty space. With the kitchen done and the workers gone, it's just me.

I throw more paste against the wall. "Until the wallpaper is done," I shout.

Kirby wanted the navy and green tartan wallpaper lining the stairs and upstairs hallway. It's a fool's errand, doing this now.

But she wanted this place to be perfect to sell. So here I am, up before the sun, to get this place ready.

"And how long will that be?"

"I dinnae know, Mum."

Mum comes into my line of sight as I line up the tartan pattern and press it against the goopy wall. I hate this stuff. It disnae go on easy and it's a pain in the arse.

But it's what Kirby wanted. And even if she isnae here, I'm going to make sure the house is exactly how she wanted it to be.

"Ye know she's not coming back, right?"

"Thanks, Mum. I know that. It doesn't mean that I cannae finish the job here."

"It's not your job anymore, lad."

"I know."

"Then why are ye still working?" she asks, crossing her arms.

Christ. I'm not ready to deal with my emotions of Kirby leaving. It's easier to be here getting this place done and keeping busy.

"Do you really want to live next door to a run-down house? It's an eyesore."

"That's the only reason ye're doing this, Cal?"

"Christ, Mum."

With the strip firmly in place, I drop down onto the hard step and run a hand through my unruly hair. It's only been a few days without Kirby, but it feels like months have gone by. I didnae realize just how far under my skin she got.

It hurts worse than when my ex left.

Christ, how is that even possible?

"Ye're a mopey bawbag right now, Cal. This cannae keep up."

"Mum, can you not just let me be?"

"Well, someone has to make sure ye're okay. Ye've been a right shite since Kirby left."

"Dinnae say her name," I snap.

"Oh yes, nothing is wrong with ye." Mum rolls her eyes and tsks. "Ye weren't like this when yer ex left."

I stare down at my hands, covered in the awful wallpaper glue. I pick at the dried paste around my fingernails.

"Mum, please."

The rain sounds louder against the windows. It's been nothing but rain since she left. With the cold weather moving in, I'm surprised it's not snowing yet.

It's like even this place misses Kirby. Even if it's always like this here, my mood just matches the shite weather.

Mum sits on the step below me, dropping a warm hand on my knee. "Cal, what's wrong?"

"Mum—"

She holds up a finger, a look of anger on her face. "If ye say yer fine, I'm going to beat ye!"

That pulls a laugh out of me as I thread my fingers through my hair. "I miss her."

"Aye. I know that, son."

"She left to go live her life and just left me here."

"Did ye ask her to stay?"

I shrug a shoulder. "She widnae have."

"But did ye?" Mum asks again.

"No."

Mum pats my knee before standing up and leaning over to kiss my head. "Ye huvnae had an easy go of it. With your wife leaving and Nan dying, ye have good reason to be wary of people. But Kirby isnae one of them. Maybe ye're finishing this place out of some misguided attempt ta bring her back, but love, ye need to move on from the past. Figure out what ye want and move forward with yer life. Ye dinnae owe anyone anything."

At that, she walks away as a rooster's crow fills the empty house.

Of fucking course.

Heading down to the lounge, I turn on the TV so he's quiet. The last thing I need is to be thinking about committing rooster murder.

My skin is buzzing, not quite sure what I want to do. The only thing I can do right now is finish this damn lodge.

It winnae bring Kirby back, but I cannae leave it unfinished. She loves it, and because she does, I'm here. Pouring my love for her into this place.

She made everyone in town fall in love with her. I huvnae been able to go anywhere without people asking after her. Even Angus and Mr. Peep seem sadder without her here.

She left. Fled back to her life in LA.

I only wish the life she was creating here was enough for her to stay. I thought there was more to her than the high-powered businesswoman.

I hoped that I could convince her to stay. That this little town, that isnae more than a blip on the map, would convince her to stay.

But it didnae. *I* didnae. I didnae even try.

I chastise myself as I hang the wallpaper, moving up the stairs into the hallway and then toward the attic.

Why did I let myself get so wrapped up in another woman again and lose myself? It happened with my business and it cost me everything. It happened with Kirby.

Mum's earlier words are ringing in my ears.

Figure out what you want and move forward with your life.

Opening the door to the attic to get the spare glue I stashed there, I remember the night I found Kirby up here. The letters her nan had written.

Without knowing it, this place has become more to me than I ever imagined it would be.

For months, I walked by it without really seeing it. Now, knowing what it means to Kirby, I dinnae think I could ever let her sell it to someone that disnae love and care for it like she did.

I want the love that her biological nan had for this place to be evident. To be splashed across the walls so everyone who comes here knows that this place is more than just a place to rest their head.

Pulling out my phone, I find my lawyer's number and hit dial. Because if I'm going to make this mad idea work, I'm going to need that money I tucked away for safe-keeping.

I was saving that money for a rainy day. For when I decided on what I was going to do in the future. Who knew that my past life would be funding my new life? Even if Kirby isnae here anymore, this is what I want. To be here in Aberlach.

And maybe, just maybe, it'll get me out of Mum's house once and for all.

Chapter Thirty

KIRBY

"I'm sorry, how much?" I stare at the agent across from me in disbelief. "I'm bringing it back tomorrow."

No sense in renting a car when I'll be here long term. I'll need my own car. But by the time I landed after taking four different connecting flights to get to Edinburgh, I couldn't really go to a car lot to drive off with a new one.

"Rentals are in high demand," he tells me matter-of-factly.

"But I'm bringing it back tomorrow."

"And ye're here on a Saturday. It's one of our most popular days."

"Fine."

I'm no longer the wide-eyed tourist I was when I landed all those months ago. This guy is probably taking advantage of me, but at this point, I don't care. I have better things to do than argue with him. I push my credit card across the counter and let him run it. I want to get out of here sooner rather than later.

I didn't sleep more than a few hours on the flights over.

Every single thing that could go wrong with coming back here kept flitting through my head.

If only I could have used that complimentary wine to fall asleep.

Will Callum still be here, waiting for me?

Will Mr. Peep recognize me?

Will Miriam hate me for leaving the way I did?

I don't know why I left to begin with. Scotland has woven her way into my soul and is a part of me. It was always a part of me; I just didn't know it.

Maybe I had to leave to realize what this place meant to me. There's nothing left for me back home. That job? I realized how much it was eating away at me. The fact that someone I thought was a friend could easily use me like that made me recognize that I don't want any part of the rat race.

With a courageous push from my mother, I knew I could come back here. Leave everything I've known behind —again—and truly make a go of being here.

Last time was temporary. This time? Everything will be permanent.

Which was the cause for my delay. I wanted nothing more than to get into my car after meeting with Ross and HR and head to the airport and get here. But I knew I needed to do it with a clear head.

I took my time, getting the necessary documents in line to become a Scottish citizen and opening all the needed bank accounts so I could operate the inn.

The Thistle Hill Lodge.

The place that has excitement coursing through me at the thought of getting home to it. Because it is my home. Maybe it was from the minute I walked in the creaky old door.

"Enjoy your trip." The agent holds out the keys, my

credit card, and the paperwork for me. I grab it with more force than necessary and make a dash for the parking lot.

"Not a trip!" I call out behind me. "I'm going home!"

I track down my car with ease, shove my two oversized suitcases into the small backseat, and get into the correct side of the car.

Now that I'm here, my nerves are starting to get the better of me.

"You can do this, Kirby. You can do this," I tell myself. It's the same pep talk I gave myself the first time I landed. Only now, it's needed for a different reason.

Driving here feels different now. Callum never showed me how to navigate the roads, but maybe because I've gone out with him, it's easier. This place feels familiar. I wish I got to know my biological grandmother, but I can't help but feel she knew what I needed more than anyone else in the world.

I found a life here. A family. My place in the world.

By the time I'm getting off on the road toward Aberlach, I'm at the point of bursting. I just want to be there.

Except the person in the small, black car in front of me is driving slower than dirt. They must be tourists, because ignoring the first passing place, they continue rumbling down the road.

"Come on!" I shout, wishing that would move them along. Don't they know what I have to do? Nothing like someone getting in your way when you have a life-altering proclamation to make.

When they pass the second passing place, me hot on their tail, I lose it.

"Move it!" I lay on the horn. I can't take this anymore. I don't have time for this.

Finally. Finally, they put on their blinker and move into a passing place.

"You numpty!" I shout, speeding around them as they let me go past them.

Oh my God.

Laughter bubbles out of me as I find the next pullout and ease the car into it. Throwing the car into park, I get out and take in the dark fields in front of me. No crashing the car because I'm terrified of oncoming vehicles.

I'm not the same scared woman I was when I arrived.

One-lane roads? No big deal.

And now, a hairy coo is striding up to the fence with purpose. I only wish I had one of Callum's sausage rolls to feed him.

"Hi Angus." He sticks his rough tongue out, hoping for what I can't give him. "I missed you."

Scratching between his horns, I know I made the right decision coming here. Even if I don't get Callum back, I'll have this place to keep me going. Because it's where I'm meant to be.

"Maybe if you see Callum before I do, you can put in a good word?"

He lets out a long, screeching moo.

"I'll take that as a yes. I'll see you soon, okay?"

Angus heads back the way he came, no doubt in search of someone who will give him what he wants. I can't believe I was ever scared of him. He's the most gentle creature I've met here. More so than that damn rooster—who I miss, believe it or not.

Getting back into the car, I speed off in the direction of Aberlach. Will Callum even want to see me? God, I hope so. I hope I didn't muck everything up past the point of fixing it.

The town comes into sight and it's a welcome relief. People I recognize are loitering outside the pub with pints in hand, even at this late hour. I pass by Fiona's, the lights still on. I recognize the person she is talking to.

It's almost like this place is giving me exactly what I need to make this happen. Finding the first spot to ditch the car, I rush over to them. Fiona's eyes widen as Miriam spins on her heel to see what she's looking at.

"Kirby! What are ye doin' here?" Miriam sweeps me into a soul-crushing hug. I return it with equal fervor.

"I came back."

"I only assumed." She laughs. Pushing me back, she rakes her knowing eyes over me. "Christ, ye've been gone for two weeks and ye're skin and bones."

I pull her back to me, because of course she would say that. "I'm fine. I promise. But I do need to find—"

"He's at the lodge," Miriam cuts me off.

"He is? Why?"

Miriam gives me a final squeeze before shifting me in her arms and patting my cheeks. She does it in such a tender, motherly way that it only reiterates my decision to come back here. Even if I'm not with my own mother, I'll have one here.

"Oh, my sweet, little hen. Ye know why."

That small sliver of hope that wedged itself inside my chest blooms.

"Really?"

"Aye." Miriam shoos me away. "Now go!"

"Poor Mary. She'll be so heartbroken that Callum is off the market," I hear Fiona say.

"Damn right he's off the market!" I call back to her.

Forgoing the car, I turn up the road to the inn and run. By the time I get to the sloping front lawn, I stop dead in my tracks. My lungs are sucking in the fresh air, but it's hard for me to breathe. Because the house in front of me isn't the same house that I left.

The stone that was looking run-down looks freshly washed. The glass in the windows that line the breakfast room is new, bursts of colors no doubt casting the room in their light.

It's hard to believe how much work has been done in the two weeks that I was gone.

Running the rest of the way to the front door and bursting through it, I see it's even better inside.

My grandma's letters hang over the wallpaper I picked out. A bright and shiny front desk welcomes me. The lounge looks equally stunning with pictures from the town covering every wall. New bottles of the whisky that Callum and I drank in here after our day on the loch sit unopened on the shelves.

Which are the original color I picked out.

It's everything I wanted for this place.

"But how?" I whisper, spinning in the room, trying to take everything in. That's when I hear the ceilings creak. I guess not everything changed.

I follow the noise. Could it be Callum? My heart stutters with every step I take. It's hard not to marvel at the transformation of this place.

Everything is gleaming. It's what I hoped this lodge would be. Not only for me, but for my grandma. The upstairs is even better than the downstairs. The wallpaper I picked out was hung with precision. I glance into each room, and they are exactly how I wanted them, right down to the shiny new beds that were going to take weeks to get here.

It's all here. Everything.

Including the mutters of the man I want to see most.

I stop in the doorway to the main bedroom, and the broad back that I see has my heart stopping and starting.

Callum.

The man who stole my heart in the place of my dreams.

"What are you doing?"

His shoulders bunch underneath the tight T-shirt he's wearing. Dropping the hammer in his hand, he turns to face me.

His beard has gotten longer. His hair is a shaggy mess, falling out of the hair tie that it's pulled back in.

"What the fuck are ye doin' here?" Callum asks by way of greeting.

I shrug my shoulders. "I had a job to finish here."

His brows furrow together. "What about yer fancy job in LA?"

"I don't need it."

"Why not?"

I watch the rise and fall of his muscular chest. Watching each measured breath he takes. "Because I want this job. This place."

"What, hanging picture frames?"

"You're such a smart arse," I tell him, a grin splitting my face.

Callum closes the distance between the two of us. His work boots line up with my own dirty work boots. The ones I wore every day while bringing this place to her old glory.

"Ye come to Scotland for a few weeks and think ye belong, is that it?" Callum asks. I watch him fight the smirk on his face.

"I think so, aye."

Callum is fighting harder not to smile. "A few Scottish words dinnae mean ye're a Scot, lass."

"So what does?" I cross my arms, glaring up at him. "Maybe the fact that my birth mom was Scottish? I mean, I have an inn on Loch Ness. That has to count for something." I inject humor into my voice. "Or, you know, falling in love with one."

"Falling in love, huh? Mr. Peep will be happy to hear that."

"I'm beginning to question myself now." I roll my eyes at him, smacking him in the chest. Callum takes hold of my hand and doesn't let go.

His warmth seeps into me, and it's everything I never knew I wanted. This man. This place.

It's everything.

"Seems convenient because I seem to have fallen for some mad Yank with crazy hair."

"Excuse me, my hair is not crazy!"

Callum smirks. "Have you looked in a mirror, lass?"

"I'm beginning to question my feelings for you."

I try to drop my hand from his chest, but he only pulls me closer.

"Right pain in the arse you are, most days," he tells me, "but I cannae seem to shake this bonny lass."

"Even when she flees?"

Callum shakes his head. "The lass came back. Seems to me she didnae."

Fisting my hands in his shirt, I pull him toward me. "It seems I couldn't shake this broody guy I stumbled upon."

Callum laughs, deep and loud. God, I could spend the rest of my life listening to him laugh and it wouldn't be enough. "You and I remember our meeting much different."

"Maybe if you hadn't scared me."

Callum wraps his large hands around my waist, and I never want to leave his hold. "I believe you were already covered in toilet water when we met. I dinnae think that was my fault."

"And the kilt?" I quirk a brow at him.

"You liked that. Admit it."

"I'll do no such thing."

Callum tucks a stray lock of hair behind my ear. "I want to get back to what you said earlier."

"What was that?"

"About falling in love with me."

I take a deep breath, ready to confess everything to him. "I did. And then I got scared. I thought my life was back in LA, but it wasn't."

"And where is it?" Callum presses his lips to my forehead.

"Here. My life is here now. With you, if you still want me."

Callum's hands drop lower before he hauls me into his arms. "I'll always want you, lass. I love you. With my entire being."

Clasping my hands behind his neck, I capture his mouth with mine. Relearning his lips. His tongue. Every cell of him that makes my heart race. I don't know how I ever thought I could live without this man. He's as much a part of me as this place is.

"I'm sorry it took me a little longer to realize it. Because I love you, Callum."

"Not as much as I love you."

Pressing me against the wall, Callum seals our confession with a life-altering kiss. The kind of kiss I will always remember.

"Not possible," I mutter against his lips. "God, I'm so happy to see you."

"You know who else will be happy to see you?"

I smile against him. "I already saw your mom."

Callum shakes his head. "Mr. Peep. He was a right pain in my arse since you left."

"Did you put on the cooking shows for him?"

"I think it was you that he loved. Not the bakes."

"So you love me and my rooster?"

Callum buries his head into my neck, the stubble tickling my skin. "Are you really going to make me say it?"

"Oh, yes."

"Fine. I love your damn rooster."

"Thank you." I drop a peck to his lips.

"Christ, woman. Is this what life is going to be like with you? You always having to be right?"

"Yes," I say, matter-of-factly. "Better get used to it now."

"As long as you're in my bed every night, I'll do whatever you ask of me."

"As long as I have you in my life, that's all I need."

The perfect life. The only life I want.

One here with Callum in Scotland.

It doesn't get any better than this.

Epilogue

CALLUM - SEVEN MONTHS LATER

"Is everything ready?" Kirby asks, a checklist in hand.

"Aye, love."

"And the bon bons?" Her eyes aren't focused on me as she makes notes to herself on the paper on her clipboard.

"Mum is bringing them over once they're done. Dipping sauce and all."

Because Christ knows we cannae make them without burning them.

"Good. Fiona dropped off the cupcakes last night," Kirby tells me without really listening to me.

It was Fiona's contribution to the night. Ones decorated like hairy coos. Kirby wanted them for the first guests, but Fiona offered to bring them now as well.

Proving once again, everyone in town loves this woman.

I take a swig of whisky from my glass as I watch Kirby go through everything we worked all day to complete. Tonight is the soft opening for the inn, as a thank you for everyone that helped make this dream of hers—*ours*—possible.

"Kirby," I call out to her before she wanders into the lounge.

"And you have the drinks ready to go?" she asks me, opening the refrigerator to answer her own question. "All set there."

"Kirby." I add a little more force to hopefully get her to listen to me.

"And the plates are all out in the lounge?" she asks.

"Kirby, love." I close the distance between the two of us and rest my hands on her shoulders. I force her to focus on me. "Everything is ready. Every bed is made and every vase is filled with the thistles you picked from the garden. The bar is fully stocked and I even made sure the TV in the coop is on so Mr. Peep disnae disturb anyone."

Kirby breathes a sigh of relief and falls into my waiting arms. The place I love her being the most. "I know you think I'm being crazy—"

"Not crazy," I interrupt. "You've put a lot of work into this place and you want it to succeed."

"You're wrong."

"I am?" My hands drift lower, plucking the clipboard out of her hand and resting it on the buffet table behind me.

"We. We've put a lot of work into this place."

"Aye." A slow smile spreads across my face as I lean down to kiss her.

I dinnae know if I'll ever get my fill of her.

When Kirby came back, I confessed to her that I had talked to my lawyers to buy this place. After she finished crying, she decided to make me the co-owner of the Thistle Hill Lodge so we can run it together.

As much as this place means to her, it means something to me too. It gave me the fresh start I needed after treading water for so long.

It has Kirby's past, but our future. We spent the last few weeks making sure everything was perfect. No nail out of place. Every piece of wallpaper hung perfectly.

The Thistle Hill Lodge is the perfect mix of old and modern.

"Thank you, Callum," Kirby whispers against my lips.

"No thanks needed, bonny lass. I love you."

"I love you, Callum."

"Can I give you your present before everyone gets here?"

"You got me a present?" Kirby asks.

"Aye. We had to mark the occasion somehow."

Covering her eyes with my hand, I steer her toward the foyer before I position her just right. Revealing the small statue to her, I wait for her reaction.

"Callum." It's an insufferable sigh. One I have no doubt I'll be hearing every day of my life. "You didn't."

"I couldnae pass him up!" The knight in shining armour stands proud next to the antique table we bought together in Edinburgh. "He has to guard the inn."

"Isn't that what you're for?" Kirby wraps her arms around me as a smile graces her beautiful face.

"Aye, but think of how much guests will like him," I point out to her.

"If they don't run off screaming. I can't believe you bought him."

I press my forehead to hers. "That day made me realize I was in love with you. That I could open up to you about my past and you didnae run. That you saw me for the real me. And I wanted to have something to remember it by."

"You know exactly what to say, Callum. God, I love you."

Kirby links her fingers behind my neck and pulls me

down in a searing kiss. My tongue dips into her mouth to tangle with hers.

"Ack! Stop lovin' on each other!" Mum's voice echoes around the room as she bursts in through the front door. "Ye have a special guest and none of us need to see that."

Kirby jumps back from me before her eyes go wide. "Mom?"

"You really didn't think I'd miss the grand opening, did you?"

"You said you were busy." Kirby rushes over to her and squeezes her tight. The woman I huvnae met sends a wink to me.

"I wanted to surprise you. That hunk of a man you got there helped me."

"You did?"

Kirby spins to look at me, eyes glittering with tears.

"I couldnae let her miss this."

I've only spoken with Irene on the phone, but she looks exactly like I pictured her. A trimmed blonde bob, brown eyes, and a warm smile.

"I can't believe you kept this a secret." Kirby shakes her head, wrapping her mom up in another hug.

"I wanted it to be a surprise," her mom tells her.

"C'mon, let me show you around."

Kirby winks at me as she takes her mother on the grand tour.

Leaving my own mum to wrap her arms around me. "I'm proud of you, Cal."

It has my eyes stinging.

"Thanks."

"I mean it." She pats my cheek. "Seeing ye have a renewed purpose—something that brings ye joy—makes me happier than ye could ever know. And finding it with Kirby? I would've disowned ye if ye let that woman go."

"Christ, Mum." I laugh. "I love ye."

"Ye better." She pats my cheek. "I love ye too."

The few people we've invited here tonight start making their way up to the house. I call Kirby back down, so she's ready to greet them and give everyone a tour.

"It's nice to officially meet you, Callum," Irene greets me with a hug.

"You too. I'm glad you could make it. Kirby appreciates it more than you'll ever know."

"She's found a new family here. I couldn't want anything more for her. I've never seen her this alive. So passionate."

My eyes track Kirby as she points out the features that we've worked hard to restore. It's the passion in her voice for this place that has me falling deeper in love with her.

I didnae think it was possible, but it is.

"I hope it means you'll be our first official guest," I tell her.

"You think I booked a place?" Irene waves me off. "I better get the best room in the house."

I bark out a laugh. "I'll be sure to put your bags in there then."

It's easy to see where Kirby's sense of humour comes from. Her mom joins in on the tour as Kirby takes everyone upstairs.

I greet the stragglers and start to get the food set up for when they return.

It's hard to believe how far this place has come. Some days, it's hard to believe we were able to do it all ourselves.

I start mixing drinks as people find their way into the lounge. When Kirby comes back down, I hand her a drink and watch as she heads to the front of the room. With the setting sun behind her, she looks like an angel.

"Thank you everyone for being here tonight," Kirby

tells them. It's the fastest I've ever seen the people in this town stop talking. "I couldn't have done this without all of your support."

I stand in the back of the lounge, letting Kirby shine. She fucking deserves it after everything she's done here. I might have helped, but it was her vision.

"I didn't know the first thing about fixing up this place, but as I learned, with the help of the people around you, anything is possible." Her eyes find mine. It has my heart starting and stopping the way she's looking at me with so much love. "And while you all supported me, I couldn't have done it without Callum. Thank you for believing in me and loving me, even when I drove you mad."

I smile back at her. *I love you,* I mouth to her.

"To the Thistle Hill Lodge!" someone yells, and everyone toasts to Kirby.

Drinks are had. Haggis bon bons are eaten. Not one single person leaves early as the night carries on well past the respectable hour to be out.

We couldn't have asked for a better night. Kirby deserves it.

Finding her with my mum and Irene, I grab her attention. "Mind if I steal this one away for a few minutes?"

"Go right ahead. Your mom and I are figuring out how best to travel back and forth once the lodge is booked for the summer," Irene tells me.

"Should I be worried?" I whisper into Kirby's ear.

"We both should." She laughs.

I make to take her out the side door, but Fiona steps up.

"Ye have quite the place here," Fiona tells us. "Elizabeth would have loved it."

"Thank you, Fiona. That means more than you'll ever

know." Kirby pulls her into a hug, and it has me bursting with pride.

This is everything I wanted it to be for Kirby. It's going to be the best fucking inn on Loch Ness that anyone has ever seen.

Linking hands with Kirby, I lead her out into the now blooming garden, bursting with color. Mr. Peep struts by.

That asshole.

"I thought you had the TV on for him?" Kirby asks, dropping onto the bench.

"I did. He just wanted to see what you've been working on," I tell her.

"Every single review for this place is going to mention the mad rooster running around."

"Better than a spitfire American."

"What am I going to do with you, Callum MacRae?'

"I can think of a few things."

Kirby smiles up at me, the stars reflecting in her soft, hazel eyes. This moment of quiet is exactly what I needed. We've been working nonstop, falling into bed every night well past midnight, to make sure this place was ready to go.

Our first guests are arriving next week. With a brand-new chef coming in from Edinburgh to take this job, we're ready.

I take a deep breath of the cool air.

"Thank you, Kirby."

"For what?"

"For coming here. For wanting to fix up this place even though you hadn't the first clue how to do it."

"We learned together."

And now we'll learn how to run this place together. The very last room that got fixed up was the largest room under the stairs. With a small sitting area, bedroom, and bathroom, it's our home away from home. Our refuge for when this place becomes too much and we need to escape.

We'll be running the inn every day. There will be a lot of hiccups, but as long as we're doing it together, we'll figure it out.

"You put me back together when I didnae realize how much I needed it," I tell her, cupping her cheek.

"Thank you for giving me a family." Kirby leans into my touch. "I couldn't have made this leap without you."

The soft light from the house casts long shadows out here. I trace her gorgeous face with my thumb.

"You would've found a way."

"You sure about that?" She laughs.

"Christ, I don't know. That first night I was worried. I didnae know toilets exploded."

That has laughter bursting out of her, echoing through the quiet night. "And yet, you still took a chance on me. Toilet water and all."

"You were pretty cute. All that frizzy hair of yers."

"Which probably doesn't look all that much better now."

"You've never looked sexier, lass."

"Mmm. Now I know you're lying." Kirby presses a warm kiss to my lips. "You know just what to say to me."

I take another kiss. It's slow and easy. Soft and unhurried. I hold Kirby to me, letting her kiss warm me from the inside out.

I don't know how this woman still has a dizzying effect on me, but I dinnae think I'll ever get used to it.

I love waking up beside her. Going to bed with her at night. The feel of her wrapped around me.

Every day with this woman is going to be an adventure.

"I still can't believe that my escape became permanent," Kirby tells me, breaking the kiss. "Aberlach is home."

"And dinnae you forget it."

THE END

Bonus Scene

KIRBY

"Is it always like this?" Crowds are gathered on the beach as the clock ticks closer to midnight.

"More or less. It's been awhile since I participated."

Callum wraps his arms around me, pulling me back between his legs and into his chest. His warmth blankets me from the cold air. The bite in the December air isn't something this SoCal girl is used to.

"I think it's wonderful," Mom says from next to me on the blanket we've spread out. "I'm so glad you invited me here."

Her smile is big as she looks over at me. She's been coming more and more to stay at the inn. *And to see Thomas.*

The two of them have been getting closer. We've been so busy at the inn, it seems like I've hardly seen her on these last few trips.

Because of the man dropping down next to her with a drink in hand.

"Pretty sure you won't be coming to visit me anymore." I laugh.

"About that…" Mom trails off.

"About what?" I shift in Callum's arms, glancing up at him to see a smile sitting on his handsome face.

"I was thinking of moving here."

"Here? As in Aberlach *here*?"

"The one and only."

"Seriously?" I'm stunned speechless.

"Who wants haggis balls?" Miriam chirps as she comes up to our small group with a silver tin in hand. "Fresh out of the oven for midnight."

"In a minute." I tuck a stray, wind-blown lock of hair under my hat. "You're moving here?"

"Oh, you told her?" Miriam asks, biting into one of the small bon bons that I love and have become a staple at the Thistle Hill Lodge. "Are you excited to have your mum here, Kirby?"

"You told Miriam before me? Mom!"

"What?" She shrugs. "I had to get her help with a few things with my visa, and I didn't want to get your hopes up in case it didn't work out."

"Did you know?" I flip my gaze to Callum.

He shakes his head. His beard is thick this winter. Something I probably shouldn't be focusing on since it woke me up this morning when it was buried between my legs.

"No. I had a hunch though since Thomas was looking more dapper than usual."

"You arse!" he calls overhead.

"Call it like I see it," Callum fires back.

The rest of them devolve into a conversation as Mom leans over to me. "You're not mad I didn't tell you?"

I shake my head and take the hand she holds out to me. "No. I just can't believe you're going to be here."

"What can I say? Us Stewarts were meant to be Scots."

"That we were."

"One minute until midnight!" someone shouts in the crowd.

"Think I can get a kiss?" Callum asks, his lips ghosting the shell of my ear. It sends heat racing through me.

I shift onto my knees between his legs and rest my arms on his shoulders. "Aren't you supposed to wait until after midnight for a kiss? Or is New Year's Eve different in Scotland?"

"Definitely different, lass." A sly grin appears under his beard. "Hogmanay requires lots of kissing. Spending the night in bed together. Waking up together."

"Mmm. I don't really recall this being a part of Hogmanay when Miriam told me about it."

Callum smiles at me and it does funny things to my insides. "Well, it's at least my plan for Hogmanay."

Smiling back at the man I love more than anything, I close the distance between the two of us and take his lips in a warm kiss.

Butterflies explode in my chest. All traces of the cold night are gone as the final countdown starts around us.

I couldn't care less. Everything I want, I have with Callum. He's been by my side through this crazy journey of opening and running the inn. Of seeing it succeed. Of spending lazy mornings together.

Until Mr. Peep decides to wake us up.

It might not be the life I imagined myself having, but it's everything to me now.

"Five! Four! Three! Two! One! Happy Hogmanay!"

Fireworks and cheers erupt all around us, disrupting our kiss. Colors explode across the sky, lighting everyone up nearby. Music rings out as couples start kissing around us.

It's something we didn't get to experience last year as we were tending to the guests at the lodge and making sure they were enjoying their own holiday.

"Happy Hogmanay, lass," Callum tells me before giving me the sweetest of kisses. A tease of what's to come. A promise that all future kisses will live up to this one.

Even if they might not be as sweet.

Just how I like them.

As the last of the fireworks cut through the sky, Callum breaks the kiss, leaving me chasing his mouth. Always wanting more from him.

"We're heading home," Callum tells everyone. There's a twinkle in his eyes. "See you for brunch at the inn tomorrow?"

"Listen ta ye," Miriam says. "Inviting us over for breakfast. Never thought I'd see the day."

"Alright, alright." Callum laughs. "We're leaving."

I give both my mom and Miriam a quick peck on the cheek. "Don't get into any trouble."

"No promises," Miriam says.

"We could say the same to you!" Mom calls out after me.

"I don't know if the two of them living in the same town is going to be a good thing." I laugh, as Callum links his hand with mine and pulls me up the trail from the loch.

"I don't think Aberlach is ready for that."

"It'll be nice to have her here," I tell him.

The town appears through the trees as a light snow starts to fall.

"I'm glad she'll be here for you."

I burrow closer into Callum's side. "I'll have everyone I love here."

I feel Callum press his lips to the crown of my head as we dodge the few people leaving the fireworks show. The gas lamps are brightly lit as we head down the main road of town. Groups of people are spilling out of the pubs, pints in hand.

Callum and I were invited out with our friends, but we wanted to have a quieter night. A small little family affair with the people I love most in the world.

I couldn't have asked for a better night.

"You know, there's another tradition that's part of Hogmanay," Callum tells me as the lodge comes into view.

A few guests are out in the yard, drinks in hand. We wave as we pass by on the way to our own private residence attached to the side of the house.

"Oh yeah?"

Callum pushes me against our front door. Business at the inn has been booming, and we've been able to hire a few people. Even with them, it's been hard to hand over control of the lodge to others. This place is my baby. I'll never *not* worry about it.

Especially since I'm now a citizen of Scotland. *Officially.*

There's no getting rid of me.

"It's called first footing," he tells me, wrapping a warm hand around my waist. Even through the layer of my sweater and coat, it seeps into me. "You're supposed to let a tall, dark-haired man into your house."

"Really?"

"Aye, lass. Said to be good luck."

I stare up at the man who captured my heart. Who I couldn't imagine spending my life without.

Grabbing the lapels of his jacket, I pull him close. Our breaths swirl in the cold night air around us. "Know where I can find one of them?"

"Cheeky lass."

Callum hefts me into his arms before opening the door and guiding us toward the small bedroom off the even smaller living room.

We spend the night buried inside one another. Loving on each other in the way only the two of us can.

Callum MacRae still takes my breath away. Being in his arms is my favorite place in the world. As long as we have each other, everything else will sort itself out.

Callum wraps me up in his arms, pulling the soft tartan blanket over our spent bodies. His beard brushes my shoulder.

"Happy Hogmanay, lass."

"Happy Hogmanay, Callum."

There's no other way I'd rather spend this holiday than here. Happy Hogmanay indeed.

Author's Note

BOOK NUMBER TWENTY IS OUT IN THE WORLD!

The Highland Escape has been two years in the making. I went to Scotland in September, 2022, and it was a dream! The people. The country. The Highlands! I loved every single minute of that trip. And when I got invited to sign at RARE Edinburgh, this book got moved up the to be written list. I can't wait to take my favorite person, Tina, with me to Scotland to show this book my favorite places <3

Thank you to my wonderful beta readers Laura and Jodi. I appreciate you more than you'll ever know (especially Laura for being my Scottish beta reader!). To all my incredible author friends, who are too many to name here…you know I love you!

To my Street Team and the Silver Society…I love getting to share my books with you and your excitement for them. Thank you to all the readers everywhere…for sharing and loving on my books and characters! There aren't enough words to thank you for your support!

<3 Emily

Also by Emily Silver

Colorado Black Diamonds Hockey

Best Kept Secret

Best Laid Plans

Best of the Best

Best of Both Worlds - coming fall, 2024

Nashville Knights

Game Misconduct - Marcus and Harper's story, coming February 2025

Dixon Creek Ranch

Yours to Take

Yours to Hold

Yours to Be

Yours to Forget

Yours To Lose

Yours To Love - a newsletter freebie

The Denver Mountain Lions

Roughing The Kicker

Pass Interference

Sideline Infraction

Illegal Contact

The Big Game

Standalones

Off the Deep End — a MM sports romance

The Highland Escape

Merry in Moose Falls - coming November 21

Love Pucked - a sapphic hockey romance, coming early 2025

The Ainsworth Royals

Royal Reckoning

Reckless Royal

Royal Relations

Royal Roots

The Love Abroad Series

An Icy Infatuation

A French Fling

A Sydney Surprise

Get the trope guide on my website, or
scan the QR code to read my books on Kindle Unlimited

About the Author

After winning a Young Author's Award in second grade, Emily Silver was destined to be a writer. She loves writing inclusive stories, with strong heroines and the swoony men who fall for them.

A lover of all things romance, Emily started writing books set in her favorite places around the world. As an avid traveler, she's been to all seven continents and sailed around the globe.

When she's not writing, Emily can be found sipping cocktails on her porch, reading all the romance she can get her hands on and planning her next big adventure!

Find her on social media to stay up to date on all her adventures and upcoming releases!

Printed in Great Britain
by Amazon